...strangled groan as if from a dis-
...whatever protest it might have sig-
...little difference to his urgent as-
...emotions.

...mated with hers. Cleo felt as if she
...g in sensation, the will to keep a
...senses as fleeting as the clouds that
...led the sun.

...he deepened the kiss, his hands slipping
...rrow straps of her dress off her shoulders.
...med to delight in the silky smoothness
...r skin.

...thin fabric dropped away, Cleo made a
...attempt to stop it. Drawing back from his
kiss, she gazed at him wildly, her breathing as
uneven as her pounding heartbeat.

'Let me,' Dominic insisted, removing her fingers…

Anne Mather says: 'I've always wanted to write—which is not to say I've always wanted to be a professional writer. On the contrary, for years I wrote only for my own pleasure, and it wasn't until my husband suggested that I ought to send one of my stories to a publisher that we put several publishers' names into a hat and pulled one out. The rest, as they say, is history. And now, more than 150 books later, I'm literally—excuse the pun—staggered by what happened.

'I had written all through my infant and junior years, and on into my teens. The trouble was, I never used to finish any of the stories, and CAROLINE, my first published book, was the first book I'd actually completed. I was newly married then, and my daughter was just a baby. It was quite a job, juggling my household chores and scribbling away in exercise books every chance I got. Not very professional, as you can see, but that's the way it was.

'I now have two grown-up children, a son and daughter, and two adorable grandchildren, Abigail and Ben. My e-mail address is mystic-am@msn.com, and I'd be happy to hear from any of my readers.'

HIS FORBIDDEN PASSION

BY
ANNE MATHER

 MILLS & BOON®

All the characters in this book have no existence outside the imagination of the author, and have no relation whatsoever to anyone bearing the same name or names. They are not even distantly inspired by any individual known or unknown to the author, and all the incidents are pure invention.

First published in Great Britain 2009
Harlequin Mills & Boon Limited,
Eton House, 18-24 Paradise Road, Richmond, Surrey TW9 1SR

© Anne Mather 2009

ISBN: 978 0 263 87456 3

Set in Times Roman 10¼ on 11¼ pt
01-1209-52623

Harlequin Mills & Boon policy is to use papers that are natural, renewable and recyclable products and made from wood grown in sustainable forests. The logging and manufacturing process conform to the legal environmental regulations of the country of origin.

Printed and bound in Spain
by Litografia Rosés, S.A., Barcelona

HIS FORBIDDEN PASSION

CHAPTER ONE

CLEO was almost sure she'd seen the woman before.

She didn't know when or where she might have seen her, or if the feeling was real or just imagined. But there was an odd sense of familiarity when she looked at her that refused to go away.

She shook her head rather impatiently. Sometimes she was far too sensitive for her own good. But there was no doubt that the woman had been staring at *her* ever since she'd joined the queue at the checkout, so perhaps that was why she looked familiar. Perhaps she resembled someone the woman used to know.

There was obviously a perfectly innocent explanation. Just because she didn't like being stared at didn't mean the woman meant her any harm. Paying for the milk that had sent her to the store in the first place, Cleo determinedly ignored the persistent scrutiny, and then nearly jumped out of her skin when the woman spoke to her.

'It's Ms Novak, isn't it?' she asked, blocking Cleo's way as she would have moved past her. 'I'm so pleased to meet you at last. Your friend said I might find you here.'

Cleo frowned. She could only mean Norah. Which meant the woman must have been to their apartment first. She sighed. What was Norah thinking of, offering her whereabouts to a complete stranger? With all the odd things that happened these days, Cleo would have expected her to have more sense.

'I'm sorry,' she said, albeit against her better judgement. 'Should I know you?'

The woman smiled and Cleo realised she was older than she'd appeared from a distance. Cleo had assumed she was in her forties, but now she saw she was at least fifty. The sleek bob of copper hair was deceiving, but the trim figure and slender legs were not.

She wasn't very tall. She had to tilt her head to meet Cleo's enquiring gaze. But her make-up was skilful, her clothes obviously expensive, and what she lacked in stature she more than made up for in presence.

'I apologise,' she said, her accent vaguely transatlantic, drawing Cleo out of the store by the simple method of continuing to talk to her. The cool air of an autumn evening swirled about them and the woman shivered as if it wasn't to her liking. 'Of course,' she went on, pausing on the forecourt. 'I should have introduced myself at once. We haven't met, my dear, but I'm Serena Montoya. Your father's sister.'

Of all the things she might have said, that had to be the least expected, thought Cleo incredulously. For a moment she could only stare at her in disbelief.

Then, recovering a little, she said with a mixture of shaky amusement and relief, 'My father didn't have a sister, Ms Montoya. I'm sorry.' She started to move away. 'I'm afraid you've made a mistake.'

'I don't think so.' Serena Montoya—if that really was her name—put out scarlet-tipped fingers and caught the sleeve of Cleo's woollen jacket. 'Please,' she pleaded. 'Listen to me for a moment.' She sighed and removed her fingers again when Cleo gave her a pointed look. 'Your father's name was Robert Montoya—'

'No.'

'—and he was born on the island of San Clemente in the Caribbean in 1956.'

'That's not true.' Cleo stared at her impatiently. Then, with a sound of resignation, 'Well, yes, my father was born on San Clemente, but I'm not absolutely sure of the date, and his name was Henry Novak.'

'I'm afraid not.' Grasping Cleo's wrist, this time with a firmness that wouldn't be denied, Serena Montoya regarded her with determined eyes. 'I am not lying to you, Ms Novak. I know you've always thought that Lucille and Henry Novak were your parents, but they weren't.'

Cleo couldn't believe this was happening. 'Why are you doing this?' she demanded. 'Why are you insisting that this man, Robert Montoya—*your brother*—is my father?'

'Was,' Serena corrected her regretfully. 'Robert was your father. He died some years ago.'

Cleo's voice broke on a sob. 'It's a ridiculous assertion and you know it.'

'It's true.' Serena was inflexible. Resisting Cleo's efforts to pull away, she continued flatly, 'Believe me, Ms Novak, when my father—your grandfather—told me what had happened, I didn't want to believe it either.'

'Now, that I can believe,' said Cleo a little grimly. 'Well, don't worry, Ms Montoya. Obviously your father is suffering from delusions. Unfortunately my real parents were killed in a rail accident six months ago or they would have told you that themselves.'

'Yes, we know about the accident.' Serena was full of surprises. 'That's when my father first learned where you were living.' She paused. 'And he is not delusional. Please, Cleo, come and have a drink with me and let me explain—'

Cleo fell back a step and this time the woman let her go. 'How do you know my name?'

'How do you think?' Serena sounded as if she was getting bored now. 'It's Cleopatra, isn't it?' And, seeing the unwilling confirmation on Cleo's face, she added, 'It was your maternal grandmother's name, too. She was called Cleopatra Dubois and her daughter, Celeste, was your mother. Celeste Dubois was one of the most beautiful women on the island.' She gave Cleo a considering look. 'I hesitate to say it, but you look a lot like her.'

Cleo's lips tightened. 'Was she black?'

Serena frowned. 'Does that matter?'

Cleo shook her head. 'Only a white person would ask such a question.' Her lips curled. 'Yes, it matters.'

'OK.' Serena considered. 'Well, yes, I suppose she was—black. Her skin was—um—coffee coloured. Not black, exactly, but not white either.'

That was enough. Cleo refused to listen to any more. If the description of her so-called 'mother' had been meant to disarm her, it had failed abysmally. She was used to vapid flattery. Usually from men, it was true. But she'd had to deal with it all her life.

'Look, I have to go,' she said, assuring herself that if there had been any truth in what the woman was saying, she'd have heard about it by now. Her parents had not been liars, whatever Serena Montoya said. And Cleo had loved them far too much to even countenance such a suggestion.

Besides which, she'd been the sole executor of her parents' estate. And she'd found nothing among their papers to arouse any kind of suspicion in her mind.

Except that photograph, she remembered now, half unwillingly. At the time, she'd thought little of it. It was a picture of her mother with another woman, a woman who she'd realised looked a lot like her. But there'd been nothing on the back of the picture, nothing to say who the woman might be. And Cleo had put it down to her own imagination. There were probably hundreds of people in the world that she bore a resemblance to.

Like Serena Montoya…

But no, she banished that thought, and to her surprise the other woman didn't try to detain her any longer.

'All right,' she said evenly. 'I realise this has been as much of a shock to you as it was to me.'

You got that right, thought Cleo savagely, but she didn't voice the thought. Nor was she foolish enough to believe that this was the end of the matter.

'You need time to assimilate what I've told you,' Serena went on, almost conversationally, drawing velvet-soft leather gloves over her ringed fingers as she spoke. 'But don't take too long, will you, my dear? Your grandfather is dying. Are you going to deny him a last chance to meet his only granddaughter?'

Cleo arrived back at the apartment she shared with Norah Jacobs some thirty minutes later.

Actually, it was normally only a five-minute walk from the supermarket to Minster Court, where the apartment was situated. But Cleo had taken a detour through the park to give herself time to think.

At any other time, nothing would have persuaded her to enter the park alone and after dark, but right now she wasn't thinking very coherently. She'd just been told that her mother and father—the two people in the world she'd always thought she could depend on—had lied about her identity. That far from being alone now, as she'd believed, she had an aunt and a grandfather—and who knew what else?—who were—well, white.

She didn't want to believe it. She wanted things to go back to the way they were before she'd decided she couldn't do without milk on her cornflakes in the morning.

If she hadn't gone to the supermarket…

But that was silly. Sooner or later, the Montoya woman would have caught up with her. And things weren't going to change any time soon. Not unless Serena Montoya was playing the biggest hoax Cleo had ever heard of.

And why would she do that? What did she have to gain by it? She hadn't struck Cleo as being the kind of woman who'd put herself out for a complete stranger. Not unless her own father *was* dying, of course. And he had another agenda she had yet to reveal.

Norah was waiting for her in the rather cramped living room of the apartment. The whole place was pushed for space, but rents in this part of London were prohibitive, and Cleo had jumped at the chance to share expenses with the other girl.

Norah was blonde and pretty and inclined to plumpness. The exact opposite of Cleo in so many ways. But the two girls had been friends since their schooldays and, despite the limitations of their surroundings, they generally got along very well.

Now, however, Norah looked positively anxious. 'Here you are!' she exclaimed in relief, as soon as Cleo opened the door. 'I've been worried sick. Where have you been?' Then, her brows drawing together as Cleo moved into the light of the living room, 'What's wrong? You look as if you've seen a ghost.'

Cleo shook her head without saying anything. Walking past her friend, she rounded the breakfast bar that separated the tiny kitchen from the rest of the living space and stowed the milk in the fridge.

Then, straightening, she said, 'Why on earth would you tell a complete stranger where I was?'

'Oh…' The colour in Norah's cheeks deepened. 'So she found you.'

'If you mean Serena Montoya, then yes, she did.'

'Serena Montoya? Is that her name?' Norah tried to lighten the conversation, but she could tell Cleo wasn't distracted by her efforts. 'Well, she said she was your aunt,' she offered lamely. 'What was I supposed to say? She didn't look like a con artist to me.'

'Like you would know,' said Cleo drily. Norah's many unsuccessful attempts to find herself a decent man were legendary. Coming back into the living room, Cleo flung herself onto the sofa, regarding her friend moodily. 'Honestly, Norah, I thought you had more sense.'

'So she's not your aunt?'

'No, she's not my aunt,' stated Cleo with more force than conviction. 'I mean, didn't anything about her give you a clue? Be honest, Norah. Do I look like Serena Montoya's niece?'

'You could be.' Norah wasn't prepared to back down. 'In fact, although you're taller than she is, you do have similar features.' She paused. 'Montoya. That's a Spanish name, isn't it?'

'I don't know. I believe she lives in the Caribbean, so it could be.' Cleo was impatient. 'But my parents were black, Norah. Not Spanish. You know that.'

She hunched her shoulders, reluctant now to remember the rare occasions when she'd questioned her identity herself. She hadn't looked a lot like her parents, and she had wondered if one or both of them might have Latin blood.

But those questions had aroused such animosity that she'd kept any further doubts to herself. And she refused to believe they'd been lying to her. She'd loved them too much for that.

'Oh, well...' Norah was philosophical. 'So what else did she say? There must be some sort of connection to bring her here.'

'There is no connection.' Cleo was exasperated. Then, seeing Norah's indignation, she went on, 'All right. She said that Mom and Dad weren't my real parents. That my biological father's name was actually Robert Montoya.' She paused. 'Her brother.'

'Oh, my God!'

'Yeah, right.' Cleo felt a sudden sense of apprehension at the sudden possibility that it might be true. 'That's why I looked a bit—spaced-out when I came in, I suppose. It's not every day someone tells you you're not who you'd always thought you were.'

Norah bit her lip. 'But you think she's lying?'

'Damn right!' Cleo stared at her emotively. 'Of course she's lying. How can you ask such a thing? You knew my parents. Did they strike you as the kind of people who'd keep a secret like that?'

'Well, no.' Norah sighed. 'All the same, I have sometimes

thought that you didn't look a lot like them, Cleo. I mean, OK, your skin is darker than mine, but you're not a blonde, are you? And you've got that gorgeous straight black hair.'

'Don't go there, Norah.'

Getting to her feet again, Cleo turned abruptly away, heading for the small bedroom that Norah had had decorated for her when she moved in.

She didn't want to consider that there might be even a grain of truth in what Serena Montoya had said. To do so would tear the whole fabric of her life up to this time apart.

She should have asked more questions, she acknowledged. She should have asked the woman outright what proof she had to substantiate her claim.

Instead, all she'd done was keep on denying something that she now saw in retrospect had to have some meaning. Maybe not the meaning Serena Montoya had put upon it, but a reason why she'd contacted her.

Dominic Montoya was standing staring out of the hotel's fourteenth-floor windows when Serena strode into the suite. The lights of the capital were spread out below him, a teeming, noisy metropolis, much different from his family's estate back home.

The door's automatic closing mechanism prevented Serena from slamming it, but the oath she uttered caused her nephew to turn and regard her with mocking green eyes.

'It must have gone well,' he remarked, as Serena charged across the room to where a tray of drinks resided on a bureau. He watched as she splashed vodka and ice into a glass and raised it to her lips before adding, 'I assume you found her.'

Serena swallowed half her drink before replying. Then, her lips tightening, she said, 'Yes, I found her.' Her blue eyes sparkled coldly. 'But you can go and see her yourself next time.'

Dominic pushed his thumbs into the back pockets of his jeans and rocked back on the heels of his leather boots. 'So there is to be a next time,' he remarked casually. 'Have you made that arrangement?'

'No.' Serena was stubborn. 'But one of us will have to bite the bullet, won't we?' She shook her head. 'Your grandfather's going to have a hissy fit.'

Dominic's dark brows drew together enquiringly, and Serena thought, not for the first time, what a damnably attractive man he was. A small core of resentment uncurled inside her. Whatever happened, her father would never blame him.

Ever since her brother, Robert, had found the infant, Dominic, wandering the streets of Miami when he was barely three years old, it had always been that way. Dominic was that most fortunate of beings: the favoured grandchild.

The *only* grandchild until now, Serena reflected irritably. Although her brother had married when he was in his early twenties, she never had. She'd had offers, of course, when she was younger. But their mother's premature death when Serena was in her teens had persuaded her that her father needed her as his hostess, and she'd never looked back.

Now, discovering her brother had had an adulterous affair with Celeste Dubois had really thrown her. She'd always thought they were close. She'd been shattered when he died. But recently, her father had revealed the circumstances of the affair, how he—and he alone—had helped Robert keep the child's existence a secret.

She shook her head and Dominic thought he could guess what she was thinking. He knew she'd never forgive Robert for deceiving her and Dominic's adoptive mother, Lily. It was the fact that Lily couldn't have children that had made his own adoption so much easier.

And he knew how lucky he'd been to find such loving, caring parents. His own biological mother had never wanted him, and she'd been only too happy for someone else to take responsibility for him.

He had once tried to find his mother, when he was a teenager and curious about his roots. But he'd discovered she'd died of an overdose, just weeks after he'd been adopted, and he'd realised again how fortunate he was that Robert had found him.

Perhaps that was why he viewed the present situation with much less anguish than Serena. OK, it had been a shock to all of them, particularly his mother, who, like Serena, had trusted her husband completely.

And it was going to be hard for her. The old man—his grandfather—had a lot to answer for, bringing the girl to their attention all these years after Robert's death. He must have had an attack of conscience, Dominic decided, brought on by the sudden discovery of prostate cancer earlier in the year.

'So why is my grandfather going to have a—what was it you said—a hissy fit?' Dominic questioned now, and Serena turned resentful eyes in his direction.

'Because she's the image of her mother,' she retorted shortly. 'Or the way she used to look before she died.' She shook her head. 'You know, I knew Celeste had had a baby, but I never dreamt it might be Robert's child.'

'Obviously, no one did. Except perhaps my grandfather.'

'Oh, yes, he knew.' Serena was bitter. 'But how could Robert do that to Lily? I thought he loved her.'

'I know he did.' Dominic's tone was mild. 'This woman—Celeste—was probably just a momentary madness.'

'A momentary sexual madness.' Serena wasn't prepared to compromise. 'Or maybe to prove he wasn't impotent, hmm?' She flopped down into one of the tapestry-covered armchairs that flanked the pseudo-marble fireplace. 'How could he, Dom? Would you do that to a woman you professed to love?'

'Uh—no.' Dominic was indignant. 'But we're not talking about me, Serena. And your brother's dead. Someone has to defend him. He wasn't a bad man, for God's sake. Can't you cut him a little slack?'

Serena sighed. 'It's not easy.'

'Anyway, I doubt if Robert would approve of what your father's doing, if he were alive.' Dominic was persuasive.

'And I dare say at the time he thought what he was doing was right.'

'Getting rid of the evidence, you mean?'

'Oh, 'Rena…' Dominic came to squat on his haunches beside her chair. 'I'm sure he had the child's best interests at heart. Her mother was dead and I doubt if my mother would have welcomed her into the family then.'

'I doubt if she would either,' agreed his aunt forcefully. 'So what makes you think Lily will feel any differently now?'

Dominic sighed and pushed himself to his feet again. 'I doubt she will,' he admitted honestly. 'But it's not her call, is it? It's your father's decision.'

'Well, I think the whole thing is disgusting. I don't know how I kept my temper when that—that ignorant girl refused to believe me.' She snorted. 'She has no idea what she's being offered.'

'Perhaps she doesn't care,' suggested Dominic quietly. 'So—did you manage to convince her?'

'I don't know.' Serena got up to pour herself another drink and then resumed her seat. 'She may think about what I've said, but I don't particularly care. She's not at all what I expected.'

Dominic's brows rose. 'Because she looks like the Dubois woman?' he probed shrewdly, and Serena turned an indignant face up to his.

'Of course, you would think that,' she said crossly. 'You're a man. Men always made fools of themselves over the Dubois women. Or so I've heard.' She sighed. 'But all right. Perhaps I am a bit jealous. One thing's for sure, she doesn't look a lot like Robert.'

'Not at all?'

Serena made a frustrated sound. 'Well, obviously she does a little,' she admitted. 'She has his nose and his mouth and his height.'

'But she's black?'

'No.' Serena shifted a little uncomfortably. 'Well, not obviously so. She's just—beautiful. Slim and dark and gorgeous. Just like her mother, as I say.'

Dominic couldn't suppress a grin. 'No wonder you didn't like her,' he teased and a rueful smile tugged at his aunt's mouth.

'Well, she was arrogant,' she said defensively. 'Like she was doing me a favour by speaking to me at all.'

'Oh, dear.' Dominic was amused. 'But let's face it, you are a complete stranger to her. She was probably suspicious of your motives.'

Serena considered. 'She really believes the Novaks were her parents, you know.'

'Well, I suppose they were.' Dominic shrugged. 'The only parents she's known, anyway. For the past twenty-odd years, she's believed she had no other relatives.'

'Twenty-two years,' said Serena pedantically. 'I guess you were about seven or eight when she was born.'

'There you are, then.'

'But didn't she ever have any doubts?' Serena frowned.

'Children tend to believe what their parents tell them,' said Dominic reasonably. 'Unless they find them out in a lie. And it can't have been easy for the Novaks either.'

'They weren't poor,' said Serena pointedly. 'According to Dad, Robert paid them a small fortune to take the baby to England and pass it off as their own.'

'There are other problems besides financial ones,' Dominic remarked drily, but Serena wasn't listening to him.

'They'd already made arrangements to emigrate,' she said. 'And the money must have been a real bonus.' She grimaced. 'I suppose the fact that Celeste had died in childbirth made it easier for Robert to escape the consequences of his actions.'

Dominic decided not to pursue the subject. Serena was never going to agree that neither her brother nor the Novaks had had it all their own way.

He doubted his father had found it easy to turn away his own child—his own flesh and blood—even for the sake of his marriage. He must have regretted it sometimes, however much he'd loved his wife.

'Well, it's in your hands now, darling,' declared Serena half maliciously. 'I've done my best and it obviously wasn't good enough. Let's hope you have more success.'

CHAPTER TWO

CLEO buttoned the neckline of her leather jacket and wrapped a blue and green striped scarf around her collar.

There was no point in pretending she wasn't going to be frozen sitting watching a rugby football match. Despite Eric's promise that they'd be protected by the roof of the stands, there wouldn't be any heating at all.

Why had she agreed to go with him? she wondered. It wasn't as if she wanted him to get the wrong impression about their relationship. He was a good friend; a good neighbour. But that was all.

The truth was that since Serena Montoya's visit, she'd spent every evening on edge, waiting for the doorbell to ring. Although it was three days now since that encounter at the supermarket, she couldn't believe the woman wouldn't try to see her again. An evening out, even at a rugby match with Eric Morgan, was better than staying in on her own.

Norah had a date. She wouldn't be home until much later, whereas Cleo's job as an infant-school teacher meant she was home most afternoons by five o'clock.

After stepping into short sheepskin-lined boots, she considered the beanie lying on the table beside her. What the woollen hat lacked in style, it more than made up for in warmth and comfort.

But, on the other hand, she didn't want Eric to think she was a wimp. And wearing a woolly hat was strictly for the birds. All the same…

With a muffled exclamation, she picked up the beanie and jammed it onto her head. She could always say she'd worn it to keep her hair tidy, she thought, viewing her reflection in the mirror without satisfaction. It wasn't easy to keep the tumbled mass of silky dark hair in check. It was long enough to wear in a braid, but she'd caught it up in a ponytail this evening.

At least no one could say she looked beautiful at present. Quite the contrary, she'd decided firmly. But then she grimaced. She'd told herself she wouldn't think about what the Montoya woman had said, so where had that come from?

When the doorbell rang at half-past six, she felt none of the apprehension she'd experienced in recent days when anyone came to the apartment. It just meant Eric was a few minutes early, and, as he only lived in the apartment upstairs, he didn't have far to come.

'Hang on,' she called, snatching up her purse and her mobile phone and stuffing them into her pockets. Then, pulling the door open, she carolled, 'See! I am rea—'

But it wasn't Eric.

In fact it wasn't anyone she knew and she felt a moment's panic. Strange men just didn't come calling this late in the day. Particularly not tall, dark men, with deep-set eyes and hollow cheekbones, and the kind of dangerous good looks that seldom went with a caring disposition.

He wasn't a particularly handsome man. His features were too harsh, too masculine, to be described in such modest terms. Nevertheless, he was disturbingly attractive. He disturbed her in a way she recognised as being wholly sexual. And that was not good.

'Um…' Her voice failed her for a moment and she saw his eyes—green eyes, she observed—narrow perceptively. Then, clearing her throat, she continued tightly, 'Can I help you?'

'I hope so.'

His voice was as smooth as molasses and twice as sensual.

Cleo's stomach plunged alarmingly. She wasn't used to having this kind of reaction to a man and she struggled to compose herself.

He had to be looking for Norah, she thought, though her friend had never mentioned meeting anyone like him. One thing was for sure: she'd never seen him before.

'You must be Cleopatra,' he went on, supporting himself with one hand raised against the jamb, and she stiffened.

His action had caused the sides of his dark cashmere overcoat to fall open to reveal an Italian-made suit that had probably cost more than Cleo made in a year at her job. A matching waistcoat was buttoned over a dark blue shirt that looked as if it was made of silk, dark trousers cut lovingly to reveal muscled thighs and long, powerful legs.

Even without the name he'd used causing her a shiver of apprehension, his appearance alone sent a frisson of awareness feathering down her spine.

No one she knew called her Cleopatra. No one except Serena Montoya, of course. Dear heaven, this man must be something to do with her.

'Who—who are you?' she got out uneasily, suddenly conscious of her less than glamorous appearance. Snatching off the beanie, she thrust it into her pocket. 'I—I was just going out.'

'I had sort of gathered that,' remarked the man, faint amusement tugging at the corners of his lean mouth. 'I guess I've come at a bad time.'

Cleo pressed her lips together for a moment and then said, 'If—if Ms Montoya sent you, there wouldn't be a good time.' And let him make what he liked of that.

The man's hand dropped from the frame of the door and he straightened. 'I have to assume you didn't like Serena,' he commented drily, and Cleo made a sound of impatience.

'I neither like nor dislike her,' she said, not altogether honestly. 'And my name's Cleo. Not Cleopatra.'

'Ah.' He glanced up and down the hall before looking at her

again. 'Well, Cleo—whether you like it or not, sooner or later we have to talk.'

'Why?'

'I think you know the answer to that as well as I do,' he replied levelly.

'Because some old man says I'm his son's daughter?' demanded Cleo tersely. 'I don't think so.'

'No.' The man shook his head. 'Not just because my grandfather says it's so—'

'Your grandfather?' Cleo felt as if the ground beneath her feet had shifted a little. 'You—you're Ms Montoya's son?'

He laughed then, his lips parting to reveal a row of even white teeth. What else? thought Cleo irritably. The man was far too sure of himself.

Then he sobered, his grin totally disarming her. 'No,' he said, and she didn't know why she wasn't relieved by his explanation. 'My name is Dominic Montoya. Serena's my aunt.'

Cleo swallowed. 'I see,' she said. But what did that mean?

'She's yours, too,' he added, unsteadying her still further. 'Robert was my father, as well.'

Cleo couldn't speak. This man was her *brother*? She didn't believe it. She didn't *want* to believe it.

'That's impossible,' she managed at last, and he pulled a wry face.

'Yeah, well, that's the way it is.' He shrugged dismissively. 'Get used to it.'

'It can't be true—'

'Cleo?'

She had never been more relieved to hear Eric Morgan's voice. The young man from the apartment on the floor above was coming down the stairs just along the hall from her door.

'Is everything OK?' he asked, coming to join them, and Cleo could tell from his tone that he'd heard at least some of what they'd been saying.

His eyes flickered suspiciously over the man standing by her door, but Cleo had to admit his words had more bluster than substance. In his navy duffel coat and club scarf, Eric was at least half a foot shorter than Dominic Montoya, and in any physical contest she doubted he'd stand a chance.

Nevertheless…

'It's fine, Eric,' she said now, grateful for his concern. She gestured towards her visitor. 'Mr Montoya was just leaving.'

Dominic knew a momentary sense of irritation. Serena had been right, he thought impatiently. Cleopatra—Cleo—whatever she called herself, was arrogant. And stubborn. It would serve her right if he and his aunt abandoned the whole business.

But she was labouring under a misapprehension if she thought his grandfather would give up. Jacob Montoya was not that kind of man.

'Are you ready, Cleo?'

The little man was annoying, inserting himself between them as if he had a right to be there, and Dominic had to bite his tongue to prevent himself from making a foolish mistake. If he wanted to speak to her again, he had to keep this civil. But the temptation to blow them both off was incredibly appealing.

'OK,' he said now, taking a step back from the door, his eyes holding hers with a narrowed insistence. 'Enjoy your evening— uh—Cleo. We'll talk again, when you have more time.'

He strode away, descending the stairs without a backward glance, and Cleo expelled a breath that was neither relieved nor convincing. She'd wanted him to go, she told herself. So why did she feel this sense of frustration? Why did she care that she'd been less than polite?

'You OK, Cleo?'

Eric was obviously aware that something wasn't quite right, but Cleo was in no mood to explain things to him now.

'Just a misunderstanding,' she said, pulling out her woolly hat again and putting it on. 'Shall we go?'

'But who was that man?' Eric asked, as she turned out the light and locked her door. 'Does he work for the education authority?'

As if, thought Cleo bitterly, and then wondered if it wouldn't be easier to pass Dominic Montoya off as someone she'd met at work.

But no, she was no good at lying. 'He's not important,' she said, starting down the stairs so that Eric was compelled to follow her. 'I hope it doesn't rain. I haven't brought an umbrella.'

Cleo noticed the car as soon as she came out of school the following afternoon.

It was already getting dark. A slight drizzle was falling and the huge black SUV idling at the kerb just outside the playground entrance did look slightly sinister.

The children had long gone, so she knew she didn't have to worry about infant predators. Just an adult one, perhaps, with his quarry already in his sights.

Putting up her umbrella, she angled it so that she couldn't see the SUV any more and, stepping onto the pavement, turned determinedly towards the bus stop. She'd timed her exit to coincide with the bus's timetable. A woman alone didn't linger long in this area, particularly after dark.

The SUV was facing in the opposite direction, so she reckoned that if her bus was on time she ought to be able to board it before the car turned round.

But she hadn't accounted for the fact that the vehicle might simply use its reverse gear. And the road was quiet enough, so it presented no danger.

Even so, the main thoroughfare frequented by the city's buses was just ahead and she quickened her pace. She didn't want to run, even though every nerve in her body was urging her to do so.

Then the car stopped just ahead of her, the driver's door was pushed open and a man got out. A tall man, wearing jeans and a sports jacket over a black T-shirt. He was at once familiar and unfamiliar, and Cleo found she was clutching her shoulder bag to her chest, as if for protection.

'Hi,' he said, apparently indifferent to the weather, rain spar-kling on his dark hair in the light from the street lamp. He came round the bonnet of the car to block her path. 'I'm sorry. Did I scare you?'

Cleo expelled a nervous breath. 'No. Why would you think that?' she asked sarcastically. 'I'm often stalked by strange men after school.'

Dominic sighed. 'I wasn't stalking you.'

'What would you call it, then?'

'I was waiting for you,' he said mildly. 'Come on. I'll give you a lift home.'

'That's not necessary.'

'Dammit, I know it's not *necessary*!' exclaimed Dominic tersely. He blew out a breath, calming himself. 'OK. What would you rather do? Go to a pub and have a drink? Or come back to the hotel and speak to Serena? It's all the same to me.'

'And what if I don't want to do any of those things?' Cleo asked, aware that the words sounded childish even to her ears.

'Oh, please…' Dominic counted to five before continuing, 'This isn't going to go away, Cleo. Your grandfather has terminal cancer. Do you want him to go to his grave knowing his only granddaughter was too stubborn—or too proud—to admit that she might be wrong?'

Cleo met his gaze defiantly for a moment, and then she looked away. 'No,' she mumbled reluctantly.

'So what's it to be?'

'What do you mean?' She was wary.

'Your place, a bar, or the hotel? It's your call.' Dominic glanced about him. 'Make up your mind. I'm getting wet.'

Cleo hesitated.

If she took him back to the apartment, there was a risk that Norah might come home early. And so far she hadn't had a chance to tell her friend about his visit the night before.

But equally, she had no desire to go to his hotel room. What if Serena wasn't there? That troubled her, too, more than she wanted to admit.

'Um—perhaps we could have a drink,' she murmured at last, and Dominic breathed a sigh of relief.

'OK,' he said, 'where? Is there somewhere near here?'

'No, not here,' said Cleo quickly, and Dominic arched a quizzical brow.

'No?'

'You wouldn't like any of the pubs around here,' Cleo assured him firmly, looping the strap of her bag over her shoulder again, almost poking him in the eye with her umbrella as she did so.

But she didn't want to have to explain to any of her colleagues, who might be lurking in the saloon bar of the King's Head, what she was doing having a drink with a—well, sexy stranger, who was evidently far out of her usual sphere of escorts.

'Where, then?'

He sounded impatient and Cleo licked dry lips before saying awkwardly, 'There's a hotel at the next crossroads. Could we go there?'

'You tell me.' Dominic swung open the passenger-side door. 'D'you want to get in?'

'Oh—yes. Thanks.' Cleo closed her umbrella without causing any more damage and climbed into the front of the car.

It smelled deliciously of warmth and leather, and when Dominic got in beside her she detected his shaving lotion also. It wasn't obvious; just pleasantly subtle. But it created an intimacy around them that caused Cleo to shift a little nervously in her seat.

'Is something wrong?'

Dominic had noticed and was looking her way now. Cleo managed a convulsive shake of her head.

'Just getting comfortable,' she murmured, far too aware of the taut fabric moulding his thigh just inches from her own.

She endeavoured to concentrate on the vehicle. It was superbly sprung, superbly comfortable, and Cleo was half sorry she was only going to enjoy it for such a short time. But perhaps it was just as well. She was far too aware of the man beside her.

Her brother!

But no. There had to be some other explanation. A surreptitious glance in Dominic's direction assured her that they were nothing alike. They were both dark-haired, of course, but so were at least a third of the population. And he owed the colour of his skin to the heat of a Caribbean sun, whereas she—

'Is this the place you meant?'

She'd hardly been aware of them moving, let alone that he'd driven in the right direction and was now slowing for the turn into the grounds of the hotel she'd mentioned.

'Oh—yes,' she said, recovering herself with an effort. 'I—er—I can't stay long. I've got a lot of marking to do tonight.'

Dominic didn't make any comment. Instead, he pulled into a parking bay, shoved open his door again and thrust long legs out of the car. Cleo hurriedly followed suit and he slammed her door behind her, pressing the fob to lock the vehicle.

Cleo had only been in the hotel once before and that had been on the occasion of a friend's wedding. The reception had been held in the conference room and she remembered lots of seafood, vol-au-vents and cheap champagne.

On reflection, she thought perhaps it hadn't been the wisest place to bring a man like Dominic Montoya. He was bound to think it was seedy and not up to his usual standard.

In fact, the lobby was encouraging. Someone had placed a large tub of late chrysanthemums on a table in the middle of the floor, and the signs indicating the various public rooms of the hotel were well-lit.

'Shall we go into the cocktail bar?' she asked, with a confidence she was far from feeling. 'I imagine we can get tea or coffee in there.'

'Tea or coffee?' Dominic's lips twitched. 'Well, yeah, if that's what you want.'

'It is.' Cleo spoke firmly. 'I don't drink, Mr Montoya.'

She started across the floor and to her relief he accompanied her. But she couldn't help being aware of the speculative glances they were attracting from female staff and patrons alike. They were probably wondering what a hunk like him was doing with someone like her, she thought ruefully.

Even in casual clothes, Dominic Montoya exuded an air of power and authority that was hard to ignore. Whereas she, in a dark green sweater, khaki trousers and an orange parka jacket felt—and probably looked—as if she was out of her depth.

Thankfully, the cocktail bar was almost empty at this hour of the afternoon. They had their choice of tables and Cleo chose one that was both clearly visible from the bar and near the exit.

A waitress came at once to take their order, not turning a hair when Dominic requested coffee for two.

'Is that OK with you?' he asked, taking the armchair opposite. 'I can't say I'm a great fan of tea myself.'

'Coffee's fine,' agreed Cleo tensely. 'Thank you.'

'Hey, no problem,' he responded, picking up a coaster and flicking it absently between his fingers. Long brown fingers, Cleo noticed unwillingly. 'So…' He arched his brows enquiringly. 'Have you thought any more about what I told you?'

Cleo hunched her shoulders. 'Yes, I've thought about it,' she admitted. She'd literally thought about little else, unfortunately.

'And?'

'And I don't see how what you say can be true,' she offered carefully.

'Why not?'

'Um—' She moistened dry lips before continuing, 'If you and I are supposed to be—brother and sister, we don't look much alike, do we?'

Now, why had she chosen that particular item out of all the things he and his aunt had told her to question first? She was pathetic!

'Well, that's easily explained.' Dominic lay back in his chair, steepling his fingers and regarding her over them with lazy green eyes. 'I was adopted. Your father's wife couldn't have any children.'

'Will you stop calling him my father?' exclaimed Cleo fiercely, even while the relief she felt was zinging through her veins.

He *wasn't* her brother.

But then, what did it matter? She probably wasn't his adopted sister either.

Probably?

The waitress arrived with the coffee and the few minutes she took unloading her tray gave Cleo time to think. What was she supposed to make of his answer? That his wife's inability to give him a child was why Robert Montoya had had an affair with Celeste Dubois?

It annoyed her that the woman's name sprang so easily to mind. She'd only heard it mentioned a couple of times and yet it felt as if it was emblazoned on her soul.

The waitress poured the coffee, and offered cream and sugar. Cleo accepted, but her companion declined. Then the young woman departed again, but not without a calculated backward glance at Dominic. Which he didn't return, Cleo noted, annoyed at herself for doing so.

Dominic tasted his coffee and then pulled a face. 'When will the English learn to brew a decent cup?' he demanded, shaking his head. He intercepted the look she cast him and gave a rueful grin. 'I bet you could do better than this.'

'I doubt it.' Cleo wasn't prepared to be cajoled into an invitation. She put down her cup. 'Why don't you tell me why you think the Novaks aren't my real parents?'

CHAPTER THREE

'IN OTHER words, why don't I cut to the chase?' suggested Dominic drily, and Cleo nodded.

Serena had been right, he thought resignedly. Ms Novak was one tough lady. And she wasn't going to be distracted by a few compliments, even if her face had betrayed a very different reaction when she'd discovered they weren't related after all.

Dominic wasn't a conceited man, but he hadn't lived for thirty years without becoming aware that women liked him. And Cleo Novak liked him as a man—if not as her nemesis. He'd bet his life on it.

But that didn't even figure in the present situation. There were enough women in his life already, and he had no intention of doing to her what his father had done to her mother. Lily Montoya was going to find this very hard as it was without him showing a quite inappropriate interest in the girl.

Nevertheless, she was very attractive...

He expelled an impatient breath and said crisply, 'OK, why don't you tell me about yourself? Before we get into the heavy stuff, I'd like to hear about your life with the Novaks.'

'With my parents, you mean?'

Cleo was stubborn, but he already knew that.

'Right,' he agreed. 'With your parents.' He paused. 'What did Henry—what did your father do for a living?'

Cleo hesitated. 'He did a lot of jobs. He was a taxi driver for a time, and a postman. When he and my mother died, they were working for an old lady in Islington. She let them occupy the basement of her house in exchange for gardening and—well, household duties.'

'Really?'

Dominic frowned. So what had happened to the not inconsiderable sum of money his father had given them? Evidently Cleo had had a good education, so that was something. But it sounded as if her adoptive father hadn't stuck at any job for very long.

Still, that wasn't his concern. 'But you didn't live with them?' he prompted and, after a moment, Cleo fixed him with a defiant look.

'Is this important?' she demanded. 'Why do you want to know so much about me? I thought you had all the answers.'

'Hardly.' Dominic's tone was rueful. 'Well, OK, we'll leave it there for now—'

'For now?'

'Yeah, for now,' he said, his tone hardening. He paused. 'I suppose I should tell you how you came to be living with the Novaks, shouldn't I?'

Cleo gave a dismissive shrug. 'If you must.'

'Oh, I must,' he told her a little harshly. 'Because whatever spin you choose to put upon it, you are Robert Montoya's daughter, and I can prove it.'

'How?'

Cleo sounded suspicious now and Dominic decided that was better than indifference. She was regarding him with dark, enquiring eyes and, for the first time, he saw a trace of his father in her cold defiance.

Putting a hand into his inner pocket, he pulled out a folded sheet of worn parchment and handed it to her. Half guessing what it might be, Cleo opened it out with trembling fingers.

And found herself looking at a birth certificate, with Robert Montoya's name securely in the place where a father's name should be.

Without bothering to check the mother's name, or the identity of the infant concerned, she thrust the sheet back at him. 'This isn't mine,' she declared tremulously. 'My birth certificate is with the papers my parents left.'

'Your *second* birth certificate,' Dominic amended flatly. 'My father bribed the authorities in San Clemente to produce another certificate with the Novaks' name on it.' He patted the paper he was holding with the back of his hand. 'But this is the original, believe me.'

Cleo felt as if she couldn't breathe. 'You're lying!'

'I don't lie,' said Dominic bleakly. 'Unlike your father, I'm afraid.'

Cleo shook her head. 'How do I know that's not the so-called second certificate?' she protested. 'Perhaps your father lied to you, too.'

Dominic didn't argue with her. He just looked at her from beneath lowered lids, thick black lashes providing a stunning frame for his clear green eyes.

And for the first time, Cleo began to worry about the consequences of her actions. What if he and his aunt were telling the truth? If they were, it followed that the Novaks had lied to her all these years. And that scenario was very hard to stomach.

Then he said quietly, 'There is such a thing as DNA, you know.'

'I don't know what to say,' she muttered at last, and saw a trace of compassion in his face.

'Why don't you take a proper look at this?' Dominic suggested, handing her the birth certificate again. 'Celeste insisted on having you registered before she died.'

Cleo swallowed and reluctantly looked at the sheet of parchment he'd given her. There was Robert Montoya's name, and her own, Cleopatra. She had been born in San Clemente, but her birth had been registered in Nassau, New Providence, both islands in the Bahamas.

Smoothing the sheet with quivering fingers, she said, 'If this is real, why did your father send me away?'

'It's—complicated.' Dominic sighed. 'Initially, I don't suppose he intended to. Celeste would never have let him take you away. But…' He paused. 'Celeste died, and that changed everything. And there was no way Robert Montoya could have claimed you as his when his own wife was incapable of having children.'

'But she adopted you,' protested Cleo painfully, and Dominic felt a useless pang of anger towards the man who'd raised him.

'I was—different.'

'Not black, you mean?'

Cleo was very touchy and Dominic couldn't say he blamed her.

'No,' he said at last, although her mother's identity had played an important part in Robert's decision. He sighed. 'Celeste Dubois had worked for my father. She was an extremely efficient housekeeper and when she discovered she was pregnant—'

'Yes, I get the picture.' Cleo's lips were trembling now. She made a gesture of contempt. 'It wouldn't do for the household staff to get above themselves. What a delightful family you have, Mr Montoya.'

'They're your family, too,' he said wryly. 'And my name is Dominic. It's a little foolish to call me Mr Montoya in the circumstances, don't you think?'

'I don't know what to think,' said Cleo wearily. 'I just wish—' She shook her head. 'I just wish it would all go away.'

'Well, I'm afraid that's not going to happen.'

'Why? Because my grandfather is dying?' She sniffed back a sob. 'Why should I do anything for a man who didn't even acknowledge my existence for the first twenty-two years of my life?'

'You don't actually know how he felt.' Dominic had noticed the way she'd said 'my' grandfather and not 'your'. 'It wasn't the old man's decision to send you to London with the Novaks.'

'But he apparently went along with it.'

'Mmm.' Dominic conceded the point. 'But what's done is done. It's too late to worry about it now.'

Cleo sniffed again. 'Is that supposed to console me?'

'It's a fact.' Dominic spoke without emphasis. 'It may please you to know that he's going to get quite a shock when he sees you.'

'Why? He knows who my parents were.'

Dominic groaned. 'Will you stop beating yourself up over who your parents were? They don't matter. Well, only indirectly. I meant—' He broke off and then continued doggedly, 'You're a beautiful woman, Cleo. I'm sure many men have told you that. But I doubt if the old man has considered the effect you're going to have on island society.'

Cleo gave him a disbelieving look. 'You don't mean that.'

'Don't I?'

She hesitated. 'So—are you saying I have that effect on you, too?' she asked tightly, a faint trace of mockery in her voice.

Dominic sighed. 'I guess I'm as susceptible to beauty as the next man,' he conceded wryly. 'But I don't think your grandfather would approve of any relationship between us.' He grimaced. 'He doesn't approve of the way I live my life as it is.'

Cleo bent her head, suddenly despairing. She had never felt more gauche or so completely out of her depth in her life.

She should have known he wouldn't find her attractive. Despite what he'd said, she was convinced he was only being polite. Besides, a man like him was almost bound to have a girl-friend—girlfriends! He was far too charismatic for it not to be so.

But she couldn't help wondering what kind of woman he liked.

One thing was certain, she thought a little bitterly. He wouldn't choose someone like her, someone who hadn't even known who their real parents were until today.

'So—do you believe me?'

Cleo didn't lift her head. 'About what?'

He blew out a breath. 'Don't mess with me, Cleo. You know what I'm talking about.' He paused. 'I want to know how you feel.'

'Like you care,' she muttered, and Dominic had to stifle an oath.

'I care,' he said roughly. 'I know this has been tough on you. But believe me, there was no other way to deal with it.'

She moved her head in a gesture of denial. Then, unable to hide the break in her voice, she mumbled, 'I still can't believe it. Someone should have told me before now.'

'I agree.'

She cast a fleeting glance up at him. 'But you didn't think it was your place to do it?'

'Hey, I didn't know myself until a couple of weeks ago!' exclaimed Dominic defensively. 'Nor did Serena. She is seriously—peeved, believe me.'

Cleo sensed the word he'd intended to use was not as polite as 'peeved' but he controlled his anger.

'Are you seriously—peeved?' she asked, again without looking at him, and Dominic wondered what she expected him to say.

'Only with the situation,' he assured her, aware of a feeling of frustration that had nothing to do with her. 'I guess the Novaks had been told to keep your identity a secret. Maybe they would have told you—eventually. But they didn't get a chance.'

Cleo heaved a sigh, and when she turned her face up to his he saw the sparkle of tears overspilling her beautiful eyes.

'I've been such a fool,' she said tremulously. 'I'm sorry. It's just—too much to take in all at once.'

'I can see that.'

In spite of himself, Dominic felt his senses stir. She was so confused; so vulnerable. His grandfather should never have gifted him with this task.

'Hey,' he said gruffly, as the tears continued to flow. Leaning towards her, he used his thumb to brush the drops away. 'Don't cry.'

He was hardly aware of how sensual his action had been until he felt the heat of her tears against the pad of his thumb.

Fortunately, at this hour of an October afternoon, the subdued lights in the lounge created an oasis of intimacy around their table, and no one had seen what he'd done.

Or, perhaps, not so fortunately, thought Dominic, hastily dragging his hand away. But not before her eyes had met his in a look of total understanding.

And he knew that she knew that for a brief moment of madness he had wanted her. Wholly and completely. He'd wanted to penetrate the burning core of her and assuage the incredible hard-on he'd developed in the melting heart of her oh-so-tempting body.

Christ and all His saints!

Unable to sit still with such thoughts for company, Dominic got abruptly to his feet. He buttoned his jacket over the revealing bulge in his trousers, hoping against hope that she hadn't seen it. For pity's sake, what in hell was wrong with him?

The waitress, ever-vigilant, came to see if there was anything else she could get him. Yeah, thought Dominic grimly, a stiff whisky. But he was driving, so he shook his head.

'Just the bill,' he said, pulling out his wallet and handing over a couple of twenties. 'Keep the change,' he added, as she started to protest it was too much.

Then, turning back to Cleo, he said, 'If you're ready, I'll take you home.'

Cleo swallowed, her tears evaporating as she became aware, in some shameful corner of her mind, that she was to blame for his sudden agitation. She wasn't proud of her reaction, but she was only human, after all. And she couldn't deny the warm feeling that was swelling inside her.

Whether he liked it or not, Dominic wasn't indifferent to her. But she couldn't—shouldn't—allow it to go on.

'I'll get the bus,' she said, making a thing of pouring herself more coffee. 'I'm not finished. Thank you all the same.'

She could hear Dominic breathing as he stood beside her. And the very fact that she could hear his infuriated response should have warned her she was treading on thin ice.

But she certainly wasn't prepared for him to bend down and pour the contents of her cup into the coffee pot. Then, slamming the cup back onto the saucer, he said, 'You're finished. Let's go.'

The waitress was still hovering and Cleo knew she couldn't cause a scene. Apart from anything else, she might want to visit the hotel again, whereas Dominic, she was sure, was never likely to darken its doors again.

Gathering her bag, she forced a smile for the waitress's benefit, and then, pressing her lips together, preceded Dominic from the room.

They crossed the reception hall in silence, but when they emerged into the damp evening air Cleo stopped dead in her tracks.

'I meant what I said,' she declared stiffly. 'I would prefer to get the bus.'

'And I've said I'll take you home,' said Dominic, brooking no argument. His hand in the small of her back was anything but romantic. 'Move, Cleo. You know where I parked.'

She decided there was no point in fighting with him. Besides, the buses were usually full at this hour of the evening, and why look a gift horse in the mouth? If he insisted on driving her home, why not let him? It was obvious from his expression that he had nothing else on his mind.

Dominic, meanwhile, was struggling to come to terms with what had happened in the bar. For goodness' sake, what was there about Cleo Novak that caused every sexual pheromone in his body to go on high alert?

It was pathetic, he thought irritably. He wasn't a kid to get a hard-on every time a beautiful woman flirted with him.

But, as they neared the SUV and he used the remote to

unlock the doors, he had to admit she intrigued him. Dammit, when had the touch of a woman's skin ever had that effect on him?

Never.

Cleo didn't wait for him to open the door for her. Sliding inside, she settled her bag on her lap, and pressed her knees tightly together. But a pulse was palpitating insistently inside her head and it was mirrored by the sensual heat she could feel between her legs.

Drawing a breath, she tried to concentrate on the car park outside the windows of the vehicle. Several people were leaving as they were, but others were just arriving.

Staff, maybe, she reflected, aware that she didn't really care. She just wanted to be home, safe inside the locked door of the apartment. She didn't want to think about Dominic, or her grandfather, or how she felt about the couple she'd always believed were her parents. She just wanted to get into bed and bury her head under the covers.

'I assume this road will take us to Notting Hill,' Dominic said after a moment, and she was forced to pay attention to her surroundings.

'Yes,' she muttered. 'But you can drop me in Cheyney Walk, if you like.'

'I think I can find Minster Court,' he said coolly and she remembered that he'd been there before. 'You'd better give me your cellphone number. If you do intend to obey your grandfather's wishes and come to San Clemente, there are arrangements to be made, right?'

Cleo's throat dried. Of course. They expected her to go to San Clemente. But how could she do that? She didn't even know where it was.

She'd been silent for too long, and with a harsh exclamation Dominic said, 'About what happened at the pub…'

'Your ruining my coffee, you mean?' she countered, grateful for the reprieve, but he wasn't amused by her attempt at distraction.

'No,' he said flatly. 'Forget about the damn coffee. You know what I'm talking about.'

'Do I?'

'Yes.' His strong fingers tightened on the wheel and she couldn't help wondering how it would feel to have those long fingers gripping her just as tightly. 'It was a mistake, right? I never should have touched you. And I want you to know, it'll never happen again.'

'All right.'

Cleo made her voice sound indifferent and he cast a frustrated glance in her direction.

'I mean it,' he persisted. 'I want you to know, I'm not that kind of man.'

'But you think I'm that kind of woman, hmm?' she suggested contemptuously, and he groaned.

'Of course not—'

'Well, forget it—Dominic. You're my brother, remember?'

Dominic wished to hell he were her brother. Her *real* brother, that was. Then he wouldn't be having this crisis of conscience.

'I haven't forgotten.' His tone was carefully controlled. 'Now, do you have that number? By my estimation, we should leave within the week. Do you have a passport?'

Cleo caught her breath. 'I can't leave within a week,' she protested. 'I have a job.'

'Ask for leave of absence,' said Dominic impatiently. 'Tell them it's a family emergency.'

Cleo gasped. 'Like they're going to believe that.'

'Why not?'

'Why do you think? They know I just…buried…my parents six months ago.'

Dominic felt a reluctant sense of compassion. 'Well, I guess you're going to have to tell them the truth,' he murmured drily, and she gave him an indignant look.

'I can't do that.' She turned her head to stare out of the window again. 'My God, how am I supposed to convince Mr Rodgers of something that I hardly believe myself?'

Dominic frowned. 'How about telling them that you've just discovered you've got a grandfather living in San Clemente? I assume they know that the Novaks came from the Caribbean?'

Cleo's lips quivered. 'You think it's so easy, don't you? But this is my life, my career; the way I earn my living. I can't just screw it up on a whim.'

Dominic bit back the urge to tell her that, unless he was very much mistaken, earning a living was going to be so much less of a challenge in the future. Jacob Montoya was a very wealthy man and he'd already hinted to Dominic that he wanted to try and make amends for his son's failings.

But when Cleo continued to look doubtful, he had to say something.

'You could always offer a few weeks' salary in lieu of leave of absence,' he murmured quietly, and Cleo's eyes widened in alarm.

'I couldn't do that. I couldn't *afford* to do that.' In the light from the street lamps outside, Dominic was almost sure her colour deepened. 'Besides, what would people think?'

'Does that matter?'

'Of course it matters.' Cleo was indignant. 'I need this job, Mr Montoya. I don't want anyone to assume I have independent means because I don't.'

Dominic sighed. 'I don't think money's going to be a problem for you in the future,' he said drily. 'Jacob—Jacob Montoya, that is, your grandfather—is a wealthy man—'

'And you think I'd take money from him.' Cleo was appalled. 'I don't want his money. I don't really want to have anything to do with him. It's only because he's—'

'Dying?' suggested Dominic helpfully, and she gave him a brooding look.

Then, when he said nothing more, she murmured unhappily, 'I suppose if I told Mr Rodgers—he's the head teacher—that I needed the time off on compassionate grounds, he might agree.' She bit her lip. 'I don't know.'

'Well, it's worth a try,' observed Dominic, deciding to reserve any stronger reaction until later. One way or another, she was going to be on that flight to San Clemente. He hadn't come this far to back off now.

'Mmm.'

She still sounded uncertain and Dominic was almost sorry when he saw the turn into Minster Court ahead of them.

There was so much more he should have said, he thought impatiently. Not least that her welcome might not be all that she expected. His own adoptive mother still lived at Magnolia Hill, the Montoyas' estate on the east side of the island, and she was totally opposed to his grandfather's decision to bring his son's daughter back to the island.

The fact that the girl was Lily's late husband's daughter had come as a terrible shock to her. She'd had no idea that the reason Celeste's baby had been spirited so hastily to England had been to prevent her from finding out the truth. Celeste's death had sealed her lips once and for all.

But it was all out in the open now, and Dominic didn't envy any of them having to deal with the fallout.

'You can stop here,' Cleo said suddenly, and Dominic realised they were outside the old Victorian block in which her apartment was situated.

And, when he did so, she pulled a pen and a scrap of paper from her bag and scribbled her mobile-phone number on it.

'There you are,' she said. And then, although she didn't really want to pursue it, she added, 'Shouldn't I have some way of getting in touch with you? Just in case I can't get the time off.'

Dominic's jaw hardened. But he had to answer her. 'We're staying at the Piccadilly Freemont,' he said flatly. 'But I'll be in touch myself in a day or so.'

'Don't worry.' Cleo's lips twisted. 'If I speak to your aunt, I won't say anything to embarrass you.'

'I doubt you could,' retorted Dominic shortly, thrusting open the car door.

However, before he could alight, Cleo's hand on his sleeve

arrested him. 'Stay here,' she said, the determined pressure of her fingers penetrating his jacket and feeling ridiculously like a hot brand on his forearm. 'I don't need an escort into my own house.'

'OK.' He slammed the door shut again and forced a mocking smile that didn't quite reach his eyes. 'I'll give you a call tomorrow evening.'

'If you like.'

Cleo pushed open the door and slid out of the car, looping the strap of her bag over her shoulder before slamming the door behind her.

Then, reluctantly aware of how vulnerable she suddenly seemed, Dominic jerked the car into gear and pulled away.

But he knew the frustration he was feeling was unlikely to be expunged by relating his conversation with Cleo to Serena. When he reached the hotel, he eschewed that responsibility and headed rather aggressively into the bar.

CHAPTER FOUR

'NOT long now.'

Cleo had been gazing out of the aircraft window, mesmerised by the incredible blue of the sea below them. But now she was forced to drag her eyes away and look at Serena Montoya, who'd come to seat herself in the armchair opposite.

'Really?' she said, knowing that 'How exciting!' or 'I can't wait' would have been more appropriate. But, in all honesty, she didn't know how she felt.

Serena had changed her clothes, she noticed. The woollen trouser suit she'd worn to board the British Airways jet in London had disappeared, and now she looked cool and relaxed in cotton trousers and a patterned silk shirt.

Cleo wouldn't have been surprised if she'd had a shower as well. The small bathroom behind the panelled door was very luxurious. Much different from the service facilities supplied on commercial transport.

But then, this wasn't a commercial aircraft.

After clearing Customs in Nassau, they'd boarded this small executive jet for the short flight to San Clemente. The jet was apparently owned by the Montoya Corporation, which had been another eye-opener for Cleo, who was still recovering from the shock of travelling first class for the first time in her life.

'Are you looking forward to meeting your grandfather?'

asked Serena casually, and Cleo was instantly aware that her words had attracted Dominic's attention.

He was seated across the aisle, papers and a laptop computer spread out on the table in front of him. He'd been working almost non-stop since they'd left London, leaving Cleo and Serena to fend for themselves.

Now he cast his aunt a warning look. 'Leave it, Rena,' he said sharply and Cleo saw the older woman's face take on a sulky look.

'I was only asking a perfectly reasonable question,' she protested, moving her shoulders agitatedly.

'I know exactly what you were doing,' Dominic retorted flatly. 'Leave her alone. She'll have to deal with it soon enough.'

Serena made an impatient sound. 'You make it sound like a punishment,' she said, flicking a non-existent thread of cotton from her trousers. 'He is her grandfather, for heaven's sake.'

'Rena!'

Serena snorted. 'Since when have you appointed yourself her champion?' she demanded. 'You've hardly said a word to either of us since we left London.'

'I've been working.' Dominic returned his attention to his papers. He shuffled several of them together and stowed them in the briefcase at his side. Then he looked at his aunt again. 'Why don't you call Lily and tell her we'll be landing in about twenty minutes?'

Twenty minutes!

Cleo's stomach took a dive.

It was all happening far too quickly for her. Despite the nine-hour journey from London, and this subsequent flight to San Clemente, it felt much too soon to be facing their arrival.

'Why don't you ring her?' she heard Serena say, as Cleo struggled to come to terms with this new development. 'She's your mother.'

'And your sister-in-law,' murmured Dominic mildly, apparently not at all put-out by his aunt's obvious frustration. 'But, OK. If you want me to ring her, I will.'

'No, I'll do it.'

With a gesture of irritation, Serena sprang up from her seat and disappeared through another door which Cleo knew led into one of the bedrooms. There were phones in this cabin but evidently it was to be a private conversation.

Or a warning?

The pilot had given Cleo a brief tour of the aircraft when she'd first climbed on board. And, as well as this comfortable cabin where they were sitting, there were both double and single bedrooms on the plane. Together with a couple of bathrooms, one of which Cleo had been glad to take advantage of.

'Don't mind Serena,' remarked Dominic now, continuing to gather his papers together. 'Believe it or not, she's a little nervous, too.'

Cleo reserved judgement on that, but evidently it wasn't a problem he suffered from.

She didn't make any comment, returning her attention to the view. She had to pinch herself at the thought that this was where she'd been born; this was where she actually came from. Was that the reason Henry and Lucille Novak had never shown any desire to come back?

She shivered, but now the distant shapes of several islands were appearing below them. And, as the plane banked to make its approach to the small airport on San Clemente, she saw the wakes of several boats moving purposefully across the sparkling water.

Her stomach hollowed again as the sea seemed to rush up to meet them, and she tried to concentrate on the sails of a large yacht that seemed to be making a run towards the island, too.

'That looks like Michael Cordy's yacht,' observed Dominic suddenly, and she realised he'd come to stand beside her chair and was leaning rather unnervingly towards the window.

It seemed such a reckless thing to do in such a small plane

that was already tilting far too much for Cleo's liking. Her hands sought the leather arms of the chair, gripping so tightly her knuckles whitened, and, as if becoming aware of her anxiety, Dominic dropped down into the seat Serena had vacated.

'It's OK,' he said reassuringly. 'Rick's a good pilot.'

'I'm sure.' Cleo licked her lips, her words tight and unconvincing. Then, forcing herself to relax, she glanced out of the window again. 'Is—is that the island? Just there?'

She pointed and Dominic leaned forward again, forearms resting along his spread thighs, his posture unconsciously sensual. Cleo's eyes were irresistibly drawn to the innocent bulge between his legs, and she had to force herself to look away.

Fortunately, he hadn't appeared to notice.

'Yeah, that's San Clemente,' he said, with evident pride. 'It always looks smaller from the air.'

'Do you think so?' Cleo had been thinking it looked bigger than she'd expected. 'Do you get many visitors?'

Dominic lounged back again, propping an ankle across his knee. 'Tourists, you mean?' And at her nod, 'We get a few. We don't have any high-rise hotels or casinos, stuff like that. But our visitors tend to like the beach life, and we do have some fantastic scuba-diving waters around the island.'

He was watching her again, and Cleo shifted a little nervously. 'Do you go scuba-diving?' she asked, and Dominic pulled a wry face.

'When I have the time,' he said. 'But since the old man's been ill, that isn't very often.'

'The old man?' Cleo frowned.

'Jacob Montoya. Our grandfather,' he said flatly. 'Remember?'

'Oh, yes.' Cleo bit her lip.

Dominic's brows drew together then. 'I should tell you,' he said, 'the Montoya Corporation is involved in a lot of different businesses. Leisure; casinos; oil. And recently we acquired a telecommunications network, that should keep the company solvent in the years to come.'

Cleo's jaw had dropped. 'I had no idea,' she whispered, and Dominic expelled a weary sigh.

'I know that,' he said. 'But don't let it worry you. No one expects you to take it all in at once.'

And wasn't that the truth? she thought unsteadily. She was having a hard time dealing with any of it. Even though the Montoyas had delayed their departure for a week to give her time to make her arrangements, it still hadn't been enough.

Not that people hadn't been understanding. Her head teacher, Mr Rodgers, had found her explanation quite fascinating, and he barely knew the half of it. Still, with his help, she had been able to persuade the local education authority that this was an emergency, and they'd given her a couple of weeks' unpaid leave.

Norah had been helpful, too, offering to go shopping with her, encouraging her to see this journey as the opportunity it really was.

'You don't know how I envy you,' she'd said, refusing Cleo's offer to pay her share of their expenses while she was away. 'You make the most of it, girl. You may never get a chance like this again.'

But, in spite of numerous good wishes, Cleo's actual involvement felt no easier. She was out of her comfort zone, she thought. Not to mention—literally and figuratively—out of her depth.

Suddenly aware that the silence in the cabin had become deafening, Cleo rushed impulsively into speech.

'Do—do you work for your grandfather?'

'*Our* grandfather,' Dominic amended drily. Then, with a lift of his shoulders, 'I guess I do.'

'What he means is, he runs the corporation,' broke in another voice sardonically. 'Don't let him fool you, Cleo. Without Dominic, there'd be no Montoya Corporation at all.'

Dominic got abruptly to his feet. Returning to where he'd

left his laptop, he began stuffing the rest of his belongings into his bag.

'Did you speak to Mom?' he asked, the coolness of his tone an indication that he wasn't pleased with her, and Serena pulled a face at Cleo before answering him.

'Uh—yes,' she said, as if there was any doubt about the matter. 'She says the old man can't wait for Cleo to arrive.'

Dominic shook his head. Serena was bound and determined to make this as difficult for the girl as it was possible to be.

'Lily also said she thinks she should make some other arrangement if this is going to be a long-term commitment.' She gave Dominic a sly look. 'She's even talking of moving in with you.' She paused. 'Now, wouldn't that be a happy development?'

Dominic scowled, and, although Cleo didn't even know the woman yet, it seemed painfully obvious that Dominic's mother had already taken a dislike to her.

'Um—perhaps I could stay at a hotel,' she ventured, just as the pilot's voice came over the intercom, advising them to buckle up as they'd be landing shortly.

Dominic gave her an impatient look as he seated himself in his own chair and fastened his seat belt. 'No,' he said flatly. 'You'll be staying at Magnolia Hill.' His lips twisted. 'Believe me, your grandfather won't have it any other way.'

Lily Montoya was standing on the veranda when Dominic, Serena and Cleo arrived at the house.

Cleo guessed she'd been waiting for them, evidently as curious to see her late husband's illegitimate daughter as she was to greet her son.

Cleo was conscious of the older woman's eyes assessing her as she stepped out of the back of the open-topped Rolls-Royce that had been sent to meet them. But then Lily flung herself into Dominic's arms, hugging him and chiding him and accusing him of being away for far too long.

Dominic treated his mother's exuberance with as much

patience as affection, his eyes meeting Cleo's over the woman's shoulder filled with a rueful resignation.

Nevertheless, it was obvious his mother had missed him terribly. And, despite his efforts to introduce her to Cleo, she persisted in distracting him with news about some woman he had apparently been seeing.

What did she think? Cleo wondered. That her son might be as unreliable towards his responsibilities as her husband had been? Or that Cleo was some kind of femme fatale, sent to take revenge on her mother's behalf?

Shaking her head, she looked about her, unwillingly aware that Magnolia Hill was even more beautiful than she had imagined. A huge antebellum-style mansion, its whitewashed facade was faced by a row of Doric columns that blended with the ornate pediment at the roofline.

Tall windows, some with iron-railed balconies on the upper floor, framed a porticoed doorway. Shallow steps stretched along the front of the building, leading up to a marble-paved veranda.

And, within the shadows of the veranda, a handful of cushioned iron chairs and a pair of bistro tables offered a relaxing place to escape the late-afternoon sun.

It was all quite overwhelming. The breathtaking views she'd seen on the short journey from the small airport had hardly prepared her for so much beauty and elegance. Magnolia Hill was quite simply the most beautiful house she'd ever seen.

The house's name was appropriate, too, she decided. It stood on a rise overlooking the land that surrounded it. A cluster of outbuildings, including cabins and barns and an enormous garage were set back among trees, while across palm-strewn dunes she could see the pink-white sands of an exquisite coral beach.

But the shadows were drifting over the island as the sun sank lower in the west and Cleo hoped it wasn't an omen. Despite her admiration for her surroundings, she hadn't forgotten how she came to be here.

She steeled herself with the thought that, in a matter of days, it would all be over and she'd be going home…

'Put the boy down, Lily.'

The gruff command enabled Dominic to free himself from his mother's clinging embrace and stride up the shallow steps to greet the elderly man who had appeared in the porticoed doorway of the house.

'Hey, Grandpa,' he said, shaking the man's hand and allowing him to place a frail, but possessive, arm about his shoulders. 'How are you?'

'Better now that you're here,' Jacob Montoya assured him roughly, affection thick in his voice. He looked beyond his grandson to where the three women stood together. His eyes flicked swiftly over his daughter and daughter-in-law before settling finally on Cleo. 'You brought her, then?'

'Did you think I wouldn't?' Dominic's tone was wry. 'I know an order when I hear one.'

'It wasn't an order,' his grandfather protested fiercely. But then he let go of the younger man to move along the veranda. 'Cleopatra?' he said, his voice quavering a little. 'You're the image of your mother, do you know that?'

'It's Cleo,' she murmured uncomfortably, aware that he'd said nothing to his daughter yet. 'How—how do you do?'

Jacob shook his head. He still had a shock of grey hair and despite the fact that there was no blood connection, he looked not unlike his grandson. They possessed the same air of power and determination.

They were both big men, too. In his youth, Jacob must have been as tall as Dominic. But now age, and his illness, had rounded his shoulders and attenuated the muscled strength that his grandson had in spades.

Still, his eyes glittered with a sharp intelligence that no physical weakness could impair. And, although his stature was a little uncertain, the hand he held out to Cleo was as steady as a rock.

'Come here…Cleo,' he said, ignoring Serena when she hurried up the steps to take his arm.

'Where's your stick?' she hissed, but Jacob only gave her an impatient look.

'I'm not an invalid, Rena,' he muttered. 'Leave me be.'

Cleo went up the steps rather timidly, which annoyed her a little, but she couldn't deny it. She couldn't help being intimidated by this man who was, incredibly, her grandfather.

She was also aware that both Serena and Lily Montoya were watching her. Probably hoping she'd fall flat on her face, she thought bitterly. It was becoming more and more obvious that neither of them really wanted her here.

Jacob was still holding out his hand and, with a feeling of trepidation, Cleo put her hand into it and felt the dry brown fingers close about her moist skin.

'My granddaughter,' Jacob said, and she was almost sure there was a lump in his throat as he spoke the words. 'My God, girl, you're beautiful!'

Cleo didn't know what to say. Out of the corner of her eye, she could see Dominic propped against one of the pillars. He'd taken off his jacket and folded his arms, watching their exchange with narrowed green eyes.

What was he thinking? she wondered. And why, at this most significant moment in her life, did she feel as if he was the only friend she had?

Which was ridiculous really. She hardly knew him, for heaven's sake. Oh, sure, there'd been that moment in the cocktail lounge of the hotel back in England when she'd sensed he was attracted to her. But that had just been a brief aberration, brought on, no doubt, by the fact that he hadn't seen his girlfriend for a week at least.

Nevertheless, almost unconsciously, she'd begun to depend on him, and it was only now that she realised she didn't even know where he lived. She knew he didn't live at Magnolia Hill.

Serena had said as much. But was he going to leave her here at the mercy of his aunt and his mother?

'This must all be very strange for you.' Jacob was speaking again and Cleo had to concentrate hard to understand what he was saying. 'I want you to know, I've anticipated this day with great excitement and emotion.'

Cleo didn't know how to answer him. How did you speak to a man you'd never met before, but who was as closely related to you as any man alive?

'I—I didn't believe it,' she offered at last, flashing Dominic a glance of pure desperation.

This had been such an incredibly long and nerve-racking day, and exhaustion was causing a tension headache to tighten all the skin at her temples.

'But Dominic must have told you what happened?' Jacob persisted, drawing her hand through his arm and turning towards the door into the house. 'I'm sure he explained—'

'Give her a break, old man.'

Dominic himself had stepped into their path, his jacket slung carelessly over one shoulder, and Cleo felt an immense sense of relief that he'd understood her panic.

'What do you mean?'

Jacob's tone was confrontational, but Dominic only exchanged a challenging look with Serena before saying smoothly, 'Can't you see she's tired? This has been a long day for her and I dare say what she'd really appreciate is a little time to herself. Why don't you let Serena show her to her room? Then she can have a shower and rest. She'll feel far more like answering your questions when she's not dropping on her feet.'

Jacob scowled, but he turned to Cleo with reluctant concern. 'Is this true, my dear?' he asked, and Cleo wet her lips before replying.

'I would like a chance to freshen up,' she agreed weakly. 'If you don't mind?'

'If I don't mind?' Jacob snorted. 'You must do whatever you feel like doing, my dear. I'm hoping you'll consider Magnolia

Hill your home; that you'll regard Dominic, Serena and myself as your family.' His lips tightened as he glanced back along the veranda. 'And Lily, of course.'

Dominic's mother looked as if the last thing she wanted to do was welcome her husband's illegitimate daughter into the family. But it was obvious from the tight smile that touched her lips, and from the fact that she didn't contradict him, that even she didn't fly in the face of her father-in-law's commands.

'Good.' Dominic sounded pleased. 'Now that's settled, perhaps Sam can fetch Cleo's bags from the car?'

CHAPTER FIVE

CLEO slept for almost twelve hours.

After that meeting with her grandfather, Serena had shown her to the rooms she was to occupy and suggested she might like her supper served there.

'I know my father won't approve. He can't wait to talk to you,' she said. 'But I think both Dominic and I are of the opinion that you need time to get your bearings before facing any more questions.'

At the time, Cleo had demurred. The sooner she got the initial interview with her grandfather over, the sooner she could think about going home. Because whatever Jacob Montoya had said, Magnolia Hill was not her home and never would be.

But it was not to be.

After the manservant had delivered her luggage and Cleo had denied needing any help with her unpacking, she'd spent a little time exploring her apartments.

A spacious living room, simply furnished with comfortable chairs and sofas, some of which sat beneath the long windows, flowed into an even more spacious bedroom. Here, French doors opened onto a balcony that overlooked a floodlit swimming pool at the back of the house, the huge colonial bed allowing its occupant to take full advantage of the view.

It had been getting dark, so she'd been unable to see much beyond the gardens. Besides, the marble-tiled bathroom had distracted her attention.

A large marble tub was sunk into the floor, while alongside it was a jacuzzi bath, with lots of jets for massaging the body. There were twin hand basins, also in marble, and an enormous shower cubicle, its circling walls made incredibly of glass tiles.

There were mirrors everywhere, throwing back her reflection from every angle, flattering or otherwise. When she first shed her clothes, Cleo spent a little time fretting over her appearance. In her opinion, her breasts were too small and her hips were too big, and she shivered at the thought of Dominic seeing her in a swimsuit.

But, despite these inappropriate feelings towards her adopted brother, by the time Cleo had had a shower and washed her hair, she could hardly keep her eyes open.

Wrapping her hair in one of the fluffy towels she found on a rack in the bathroom, she dragged her suitcase across the floor and extracted a bra and panties. Then, stretching out on the satin luxury of the bedspread, she closed her eyes.

She awakened to fingers of sunlight finding their way between the slats of the window blind. It was evidently morning, but for a moment she couldn't remember where she was. Only that the bed, and most particularly the room, were unfamiliar.

Then her memory reasserted itself, and, unable to suppress a little gasp of dismay, she pushed herself up on her elbows and looked about her.

Her first realisation was that someone had been into her room while she was sleeping. The bedspread she'd been lying on had been drawn back and she was now covered with a fine Egyptian cotton sheet. Also, the blinds hadn't been drawn when she'd lain down on the bed. So who had checked up on her?

One of the servants, perhaps? Or Serena? She wouldn't put it past the older woman to want to satisfy herself that Cleo wasn't going to appear again that night. But what had she told Jacob Montoya? Had she let him think that Cleo had chosen to go to bed rather than spend the evening with him?

She sighed. It was too late now to worry about such a pos-

sibility. And her grandfather—she was amazed at how easily
the word came to her mind—had said to treat the place as her
home. Not that she would. As she'd thought the night before,
she could only ever be a visitor here. Too many things had
happened to consider anything else.

Sliding her legs out of bed, Cleo got to her feet and was
relieved to find she felt totally rested. If a little sticky, she
conceded, aware that, despite the air conditioning, moving
brought a film of moisture to her skin. Beyond the windows,
the sun was evidently gaining in strength. What time was it?
she wondered. And where had she left her watch?

She eventually found it in the bathroom. She'd adjusted the
time on the plane and she saw now that it was barely seven
o'clock. Nudging the bedroom blind aside, she peered through
the French windows. It was a glorious morning and, despite
herself, she felt her spirits rise.

There didn't appear to be anyone about and, unlatching the
window, she pushed it open. Warmth flooded into the room and
with it came the tantalising scent of tropical blossoms and the
unmistakable tang of the sea.

She saw now that beyond the gardens was the beach she'd
glimpsed so briefly on her arrival. Feathery palm trees framed
the blue waters of the Atlantic, a frill of foam creaming along
the shore.

Slipping between the vertical blinds, she stepped out onto
the balcony. Below her, the swimming pool sparkled in the
sunlight, tubs of shrubs and hibiscus and oleander marking the
curve of a patio that was half-hidden from her view.

A maid appeared with a watering can, evidently intent on
her task, and although Cleo was inclined to step back inside she
resisted the impulse. After all, her bra and panties were no
more revealing than a bikini. It was amazing, she could stand
here in the sunlight, when it had been wet and cloudy yesterday morning in London.

She wondered what time her grandfather got up. Whether
he'd expect her to join him for breakfast. Her nerves jangled a

little at the prospect, though from what she'd seen the night before, he didn't seem a very intimidating figure.

Unlike Dominic…

Her pulse quickening, she wondered if Dominic had stayed the night at Magnolia Hill. Had he ever lived here at all? He'd told her his parents had had their own house when he'd explained about Celeste—her mother. Goose pimples feathered her skin at the memory.

But still, she couldn't stop thinking about where he might be at this moment. Perhaps he lived with his girlfriend, though that thought was less easy to engage. Whatever, it was really no concern of hers, so she should just get over it. Before she saw him again and let him guess how she felt…

A shadow moved at the far side of the pool.

For the first time, she noticed that there were cabanas there; small cabins where a person using the pool could change their clothes.

A man had emerged from one of the cabanas. A tall man, bare-chested, with a towel draped around his neck. He was wearing swimming shorts that barely skimmed his hip bones. Wet shorts that clung to every corded sinew.

As she watched, he used the towel to dry his hair, and she saw the growth of dark hair beneath his arms and arrowing down his chest. His skin was brown and sleek with muscle, his stomach flat above long, powerful legs.

Cleo's palms were suddenly damp. She didn't have to wonder any longer about Dominic. He'd obviously been swimming. But how long had he been there? And was he able to see her?

Her throat drying, Cleo eased herself back into her bedroom. Then, allowing the blinds to fall back into place, she took a moment to calm her racing heart. Wherever he lived he'd evidently spent the night at Magnolia Hill, she thought breathlessly. Would he be joining his grandfather for breakfast, too?

She was spending far too much time speculating about

Dominic Montoya. Impatient with herself, Cleo smoothed her palms down her thighs and knelt beside her suitcase.

What to wear? That was the problem. Well, not a bikini, she assured herself, with another glance in the mirror. The tank suit Norah had persuaded her to buy was probably going to remain unworn in her case.

Half an hour later, she emerged from the bathroom in narrow-legged lemon shorts and a white cotton T-shirt. Smart, but casual, she thought, remembering something else Norah had told her. It wasn't cool to look overdressed.

Besides, the last thing she wanted was for anyone to get the impression that she was looking for admiration. Or sex, she added grimly, abruptly recalling the last months of her mother's life.

She decided she could hardly blame Lily Montoya for being hostile. After all, her husband had had an affair with Celeste. But as for her being attracted to her adopted brother... Cleo sucked in a breath. There was no way history was going to repeat itself.

Her hair was still a little wet, so she found an elasticated band in her bag and looped it up in a ponytail. Then, stepping into thonged sandals, she checked her appearance once more before opening her door.

The place seemed very quiet. Without the knowledge that there were at least half a dozen servants working in the house, she might have thought she and Dominic were its only occupants.

She blew out a breath, inwardly chiding herself. She had to stop punctuating every thought with Dominic. He meant nothing to her. How could he? She hardly knew him. And it went without saying that she meant nothing to him.

A long hallway with a window at the end led to the staircase. However, before reaching the downward curve of a scrolled iron banister, the landing opened out into a pleasant sitting area. From here, it was possible to overlook the lower foyer, circular leaded windows allowing sunlight to stream into the stairwell.

As Cleo started down, she saw the huge potted fern that filled the turn of the staircase. Tendrils of greenery clung to the iron and brushed her fingers as she passed. There was something almost sensual about its twining fronds, she mused ruefully. Or perhaps she was just extra-sensitive this morning.

Certainly, she had climbed this staircase the night before. But then, exhaustion, and a certain amount of tension, had clouded her view. Not that she was any less tense this morning, she thought, pausing to admire the view from an arching window. Even the sight of the alluring shoreline couldn't quite rid her of the feeling that she shouldn't be here.

A West Indian maid appeared below her. She looked up at her with expectant eyes, and Cleo wondered what she was thinking. 'Can I help you, Ms Novak?' she asked, and Cleo was relieved to find she hadn't been introduced to the staff as Cleo Montoya.

'Um—you could tell me if Mr Montoya is up yet,' she said, deciding she might as well be proactive. If her grandfather wanted to see her, there was no point in her dragging her heels.

The maid gestured across the delicately patterned tiles of the foyer. 'Mr Dominic is having breakfast on the terrace,' she said politely. 'You like I should show you the way?'

'Oh—no.' Cleo had no desire to spend any more time with Dominic than she had to. 'I meant—Mr Montoya Senior. What time does he usually get up?'

'Your grandfather has breakfast in his room at about seven a.m.,' remarked a disturbingly familiar voice from behind her. Cleo turned to find Dominic standing in the arched entry to the adjoining room. 'He'll be down later.'

Thankfully, he was dressed now. Albeit in khaki cargo shorts and a tight-fitting black T-shirt that exposed taut muscles and a wedge of brown flesh at his waist.

Which seemed far too casual to her way of thinking. It was easier to keep him at arm's length in a formal suit and tie.

He had evidently heard their voices and come to investigate. The acoustics in the foyer must have allowed the sound to circulate around the ground-floor rooms. Cleo realised belatedly that she should have thought of that.

However, the maid turned towards him with evident enthusiasm. 'Ms Novak was just lookin' for Mr Jacob, sir,' she said, sashaying towards him, hips swinging, arms akimbo. 'You want more coffee, Mr Dominic? You do, just say the word and Susie'll get it for you.'

Dominic's lips tightened as he saw Cleo's reaction to the implied intimacy of the girl's words, and there was an edge to his voice when he said, 'You can get Ms Novak some breakfast instead. Fruit, cereal, rolls, coffee.' He arched his brows at Cleo. 'Does that about cover it?'

'I…' Cleo had hardly heard what he'd said and now she struggled to answer him. 'I—I guess so,' she muttered. 'Thank you.'

'No problem.' Dominic turned once more to the maid. 'On the terrace, Susie. As quick as you can, right?'

Susie pursed sulky lips, but she knew better than to argue that it wasn't her job to serve meals when she'd already offered to get him fresh coffee.

'Yes, sir,' she said tersely, her hands dropping to her sides as she marched away, and Cleo hoped she hadn't made another enemy.

Meanwhile, Dominic was trying to master his own frustration. Dammit, Cleo probably thought he exercised some medieval droit de seigneur over the female members of the household staff and it irritated the hell out of him.

Not that it mattered what Cleo thought, he reminded himself.

Only it did.

'Did you sleep well?'

Dominic gestured for her to come and join him and, although she would have preferred to make her own way, Cleo had little choice but to obey him.

'Very well,' she responded, making sure she didn't brush

against him as she preceded him into the room behind him. 'I'm sorry if your grandfather expected me to join him yesterday evening, but I'm afraid I just flaked out.'

'I know.'

Dominic was far too sure of himself, and Cleo gave him a wary look.

'You know?'

'Yeah.' He nodded. 'Serena had one of the maids check up on you.' He grimaced. 'You could have fallen asleep in the bath. We wouldn't want you to drown yourself before you had a chance to get to know us.'

Cleo pressed her lips together. 'I wasn't likely to do that,' she said, but Dominic only gave her a wry smile.

'All the same…' he murmured lightly. 'The old man would never have forgiven himself if anything had happened to you.'

'Just the old man?' Cleo found herself saying provocatively, and saw the way Dominic's expression darkened.

'Don't play games with me, Cleo,' he said warningly. 'You're not equipped to deal with the fallout.'

Cleo's lips parted, but she didn't say anything more. Her face flaming, she turned away, grateful to transfer her attention to less disquieting subjects.

But he was right, she thought. She wasn't used to provoking anyone, least of all a man who always seemed to bring out the worst—or was it the bitch?—in her.

It was quite a relief to study her surroundings.

Darkly upholstered sofas and chairs stood out in elegant contrast to the backdrop of pale walls and even paler wooden floors.

Long windows, some of them open to admit the delicious breeze off the ocean, boasted filmy drapes that moved seductively in the morning air.

'We'll go outside,' said Dominic after a moment, and Cleo realised he had crossed the room and was now standing by French doors that opened onto a stone terrace.

She followed, as slowly as she dared, taking in the exquisite appointments of the room. Low tables; cut-glass vases filled with flowers; thick candles in chunky silver holders.

There was even a grand piano, its lid lifted, hidden away in one corner of the enormous apartment. And dramatic oil paintings in vivid colours that added their own particular beauty to the walls.

'You have a beautiful home,' she said a little stiffly, wanting to restore some semblance of normality, but Dominic's lips only twisted rather mockingly at her words.

'It's not my home,' he reminded her carelessly, stepping aside to let her pass him. 'But I'm sure your grandfather is hoping you'll make it yours.'

Cleo's jaw dropped. 'You're not serious!'

'What about?' Dominic ignored her startled expression. 'I assure you, I do have my own house a couple of miles from here on Pelican Bay.'

'No—' Cleo was almost sure he was deliberately misunderstanding her '—that's not what I meant.'

They'd emerged onto the terrace now and Cleo could see where a tumble of pink and white bougainvillea hid the low wall that separated the paved patio from the pool.

She was briefly silenced by the view. By the pool, shimmering invitingly; by the rampant vegetation and flowering trees that surrounded it; by the ever-constant movement of the ocean beyond the rolling dunes.

Aware of Dominic's silence, she turned to him and said, 'About my grandfather—he doesn't really expect me to stay here, does he?'

Dominic shrugged, his compassion reluctantly stirred by her obvious confusion. 'It's what he wants,' he said simply. 'I think he's hoping to make up for all those years when he didn't know you.'

Cleo chewed on her lower lip. 'But why now?'

Dominic sauntered towards a circular table set in the shade of a brown and cream striped canopy. Then, picking up his coffee, he glanced at her over his shoulder. 'Why do you think?'

Cleo groped for a convincing answer. 'Because he's ill?'

'Because he's dying,' Dominic amended flatly. 'Because he's been forced to face the fact of his own mortality.' He paused. 'According to his lawyer, he's been looking for you for some time.'

Cleo frowned. 'And did—did my mother and father know this?'

'The Novaks?' Dominic shrugged. 'I shouldn't think so.'

He raised his cup to his lips and swallowed the remainder of his coffee, his dark head tilted back, the brown column of his throat moving rhythmically.

Cleo was unwillingly fascinated, but she managed to drag her eyes away and say, 'So—he waited until they were dead?'

Dominic lowered his cup to its saucer and regarded her resignedly. 'What are you saying? You think the old man had something to do with their deaths?'

'Heavens, no.' Cleo was horrified. 'They died in a train crash, you know that.' She hesitated, and then went on a little emotionally, 'They'd been to visit some friends who'd relocated to North Wales and were on their way back. Apparently the train became derailed at a crossing. It was an accident. A terrible accident.' Her voice broke then. 'I miss them so much.'

'I'm sure you do.'

The sympathy in Dominic's voice was almost her undoing, but she managed to hold herself together.

Dominic, meanwhile, was having a hard time controlling the urge he had to comfort her. But he hadn't forgotten what happened when he touched her. How uncontrollable his own reaction could be.

'Anyway,' she went on, unaware of his agitation, 'your aunt said that was when—when he decided to contact me.'

'Yeah.' Dominic sucked in a breath. 'He'd known the Novaks wouldn't take kindly to any intervention from him. But after—well, after the funeral, he had a firm of investigators find out all about you.'

'But how did he know about the train crash?'

'Again, according to his lawyer, he'd already traced the Novaks to Islington. It wasn't until after the funeral he discovered that you weren't living with them.'

Cleo frowned. 'I moved out a couple of years ago, when Mom and Dad went to live with Mrs Chapman. I was just finishing college and I'd got the job at St Augustine's, so I didn't want to move away.'

'So you decided to share an apartment with a friend?'

'More or less.'

Dominic realised she was unaware of it, but this was the first time she'd been totally relaxed with him.

And he was enjoying her company far too much.

Nevertheless, it was impossible to ignore the fact that he was possibly her only ally here. His grandfather had his own agenda, no doubt, but both Serena and his mother resented her. That went without saying.

And her vulnerability stirred him in a way he'd never felt before. In her simple T-shirt and shorts, her dark hair caught up in a ponytail, she looked so young and—dammit, innocent.

He scowled. He had to stop feeling responsible for her, he told himself. The old man wouldn't like it; wouldn't like the idea that she depended on Dominic and not himself.

But it was that sense of responsibility that had made Dominic accept his grandfather's invitation to stay the night at Magnolia Hill. Despite the fact that Sarah Cordy, his current girlfriend, had made him promise to go and see her as soon as he got back…

'Norah—that's the girl I live with,' Cleo was saying now, completely unaware of his frustration, 'she was finding the rent of the apartment too much for just one person, so she offered me the chance to share.' She smiled disarmingly. 'I jumped at it.'

'And Eric? Where does he fit in?'

Dominic heard the words leave his lips with a feeling of incredulity. Dammit, whoever Eric was, it was nothing to do with him. But it was too late to take them back now.

'Eric?' Cleo's lips rounded. 'Oh, yes, you met Eric, didn't you?' A teasing smile tilted her mouth. 'Did he scare you?'

'Are you kidding me?'

Dominic had answered without thinking, but now he realised she'd just been baiting him.

'Oh, yeah, very clever,' he grunted. 'The guy really had me quaking at the knees.'

'And they're such nice knees, aren't they?' Cleo giggled, stepping back to get a better look. 'Mmm, you definitely wouldn't win any knobbly-knees contest.'

'Any what?' he was demanding, advancing on her half threateningly, when they both became aware that they were no longer alone.

His mother was standing at the far side of the terrace, amazingly holding the tray that contained Cleo's breakfast in her hands.

Her blue eyes were glacial as they rested on Cleo's flushed face. Then warmed slightly when they moved to her son.

'Am I interrupting?' she asked, indicating the tray. 'I intercepted Susie in the foyer and she said you'd asked for this, Dominic.' Her smile was thin. 'I thought you'd already had breakfast.'

'I have.'

Dominic was fairly sure the tray wasn't all his mother had got from Susie, but he kept his thoughts to himself.

'It's Cleo's breakfast,' he said pleasantly. 'Here.' He went towards her. 'Let me take it from you.'

'I can manage,' she said.

But somehow—Dominic didn't want to think it was deliberate—the tray slipped from her hands.

Cleo jumped back as cups and saucers shattered on the stone paving, Fruit juice and hot coffee splashed in all directions, the latter burning as it touched her bare feet.

She bent automatically to pick up a rolling peach, its skin as soft as her own, thought Dominic savagely. But bruised now, as she was, by his mother's careless hands.

Then her eyes moved anxiously to his and he turned to give his mother an enigmatic look.

'Oh, dear me!' Lily Montoya pressed her clasped hands to her breast. 'I'm so clumsy.'

And if Cleo hadn't seen the look the woman had cast her earlier, she might have believed she meant it.

CHAPTER SIX

'IT DOESN'T matter.' Dominic was dismissive, almost as if destroying an expensive porcelain coffee service was of no matter. 'I'll get Susie to bring another tray.'

'Oh, please, don't!'

Cleo's cry arrested him. She didn't think she could bear to be alone with Lily Montoya at this moment.

She hadn't asked to come here, she told herself as the other woman's expression hardened. And, although she had sympathy for Lily's feelings, Dominic's mother shouldn't blame her because her husband hadn't been able to keep his trousers zipped.

'Cleo—' Dominic began, when the clatter of a stick against stone made them all turn.

'Dom! Dom!' Jacob Montoya stumped heavily across the terrace, sharp eyes taking in the scene and finding it wanting. 'What's going on here, boy? Has your mother been throwing china around again?'

'I dropped the tray, Jacob.' Lily was defensive. 'I'm not in the habit of breaking things.'

'If you say so.' Jacob spoke indifferently. 'I just hope you're not trying to intimidate our guest.'

Lily's lips tightened. '*Your* guest, Jacob. Not mine. Or Dominic's.'

'Ma!' Dominic intervened now, aware that Cleo's face was rapidly losing all colour. 'Can't you see, Cleo had no part in

Dad's defection? You can't blame her for something she knew nothing about.'

'And that's the truth,' broke in his grandfather staunchly, but Lily wasn't listening to him.

Taking a handkerchief out of her handbag, she held it to her nose, her eyes seeking Dominic's in mute appeal. 'I'm not to blame either,' she whispered tearfully. 'I thought you would understand how I felt.'

'I do.' Dominic could feel himself weakening, but he knew deep inside that his mother was far more capable of manipulating the situation to her own ends than Cleo. 'Just cool it, hmm, Ma? We all need to learn to get along together, right?'

Lily sniffed. 'I think you're asking too much, Dominic. This is my home—'

'But it's my house,' Jacob Montoya interrupted, his voice surprisingly forceful. 'And so long as I own Magnolia Hill, I'll say who can or can't stay here.'

Cleo stifled a groan. She pressed cold hands to her face, wishing the paving stones of the terrace would just open up and swallow her.

This was so much worse than she'd anticipated. She'd been anxious about Dominic's mother, of course, but she'd never expected the woman to take such an instantaneous dislike to her.

And the fact that Lily lived here, at Magnolia Hill, just emphasised the problem. Someone should have warned her about this before she agreed to come here.

'Look, we're upsetting Cleo,' said Dominic impatiently, and his mother let out a wounded cry.

'You're upsetting *me*, Dominic,' she protested, her eyes wide and indignant. 'But that doesn't matter, apparently.'

'Oh, please…' Cleo couldn't take any more of this. She looked from her grandfather to Dominic and then back again. 'I—I never wanted to stay here. And I certainly don't want to upset anyone. I'd be much happier if I could just find a room at a bed-and-breakfast—'

'Forget it!'

Before Dominic could voice his own protest, his grandfather had intervened.

'You're staying here, girl,' Jacob said flatly. 'That's a given. And if my daughter-in-law isn't happy with that, then I suggest she finds somewhere else to stay, not you.'

'Oh, but—' began Cleo, only to have Dominic intercede this time.

'Would you rather Cleo stay at Turtle Cove with me, Ma?' he suggested, and, as he'd expected, his mother couldn't hide her dismay at this proposal.

'That—that would be totally inappropriate!' she exclaimed, aghast, and Jacob actually laughed.

'Good move, Dom,' he said, before shuffling across the terrace to where Cleo was standing and throwing a reassuring arm about her shoulders. 'It'll all work out, you'll see,' he added, giving her a protective squeeze. 'So we'll hear no more about bed-and-breakfasts, OK?'

Cleo wanted to move out of his embrace. Whatever he said, she'd never feel at home here. But she had the feeling she was supporting Jacob as much as he was supporting her, so she merely shook her head.

'Now,' he went on cheerfully, 'I'm guessing that was your breakfast that ended up on the ground, am I right?' Her expression gave him her answer, and he nodded. 'Good. Then we'll have breakfast together.'

'You've had breakfast, Father.'

Lily wasn't going to give in without a fight, it seemed, but Jacob only gave her a warning look. 'I can have two breakfasts, can't I?' he demanded. Then he looked at Cleo again. 'But I think we'll have it in the morning room. This place needs cleaning up and the atmosphere doesn't suit me at the moment.'

Dominic watched Cleo and Jacob make their way across the terrace and into the house. Then he turned to look at his mother.

'You OK?'

'Like you care.' Lily was near to tears.

'Of course I care,' said Dominic heavily. 'But antagonising the old man isn't going to do you any good.' He paused. 'She's his granddaughter. She has every right to be here, and you know that.'

Lily pursed her lips. 'You like her, don't you?'

'Uh—yeah.' Dominic was wary. 'She's my adoptive sister. What's not to like?'

'Correction, she's your father's by-blow,' retorted Lily angrily. 'She's not related to us by any means whatsoever.'

'OK.' Dominic closed his eyes for a moment. 'But she's still a Montoya, in everything but name. Whatever names you choose to call her, she's still the legitimate heir to Magnolia Hill.'

Lily's lips parted. 'Did your grandfather tell you that?' she asked, appalled.

'No.' Dominic didn't know what the old man might decide about the house. 'But she does have a place here, Ma. Goodness knows, it was hard enough to persuade her to come.'

Lily frowned. 'You're joking!'

'No, I'm not.' Dominic was weary of this. 'Look, I've got to go. I promised Josh I'd call into the office as soon as I got back.'

'Oh, yes, it's all right for you, isn't it?' muttered Lily resentfully. 'My father left you God knows how many millions, and Jacob's already given you virtual control of the Montoya Corporation. Whereas I—I—'

'Can do exactly what you like,' Dominic interrupted her flatly. 'You chose to come and live here when Dad died. But there's nothing stopping you from buying another house.'

Lily gasped. 'This is my home!' She straightened her shoulders. 'I never thought I'd hear you say otherwise.'

'I'm not saying otherwise,' protested Dominic, wishing he'd never started this. 'I just want you to be happy.'

'Then you should never have brought that girl here,' declared his mother forcefully. 'I don't know what Sarah's going to think.'

'Sarah's not my keeper, Ma!'

'No, but she is your girlfriend, Dominic. She deserves some loyalty, don't you think? Or are you blinded by this other young woman's doubtful charms?'

Dominic stifled an oath. 'You're exaggerating the situation,' he said harshly. 'Sarah's a friend, that's all. I'll go and see her in my own good time.'

'I think she thinks she's rather more than that,' said his mother tightly. 'But in any event, I'd make my peace with her before she hears about your apparent attachment for your grandfather's—um—folly—from someone else.'

Dominic scowled. 'What the hell is that supposed to mean?'

'You can't deny you and the Novak girl were acting very cosy when I walked onto the terrace,' Lily asserted, pushing the tissue she'd been using back into her bag.

Dominic raked long fingers through his hair. 'Don't call her the Novak girl!' he exclaimed frustratedly. 'Anyway, what do you mean, we were acting cosy? What did you *think* we were doing?'

'I don't know, do I?'

'Oh, for pity's sake!' Dominic was rapidly losing his temper and it was an effort to rein it in. 'I was trying to get her to relax, that's all. If you'd get your head out of your—' He broke off, before he said something unforgivable, and continued, 'Get to know her, Ma. You might like her, too.'

'I don't think so.'

Lily was inflexible and Dominic gave up. 'I'm going to change,' he said. 'I need to get into town.'

Hunched shoulders was his only answer and, blowing out an impatient breath, Dominic started for the door.

There was no point in saying any more, he realised. He'd probably said more than he should already. But, dammit, Cleo needed someone other than his grandfather to fight her corner.

Breakfast with her grandfather was surprisingly enjoyable.

And, although Cleo knew it was due in no small part to

Jacob's determination to put her at her ease, she found him amazingly easy to talk to.

Much like Dominic, she admitted unwillingly. Except that when she was talking to her grandfather, there was no sexual tension between them.

As there was with Dominic.

A shiver of remembrance prickled her spine. She didn't know what might have happened if his mother hadn't interrupted them as she had. Or was that simmering awareness between them only in her mind, not his? There was no doubt it played an integral part in the way she reacted to him.

But it was pleasant, sitting in the sunlit luxury of the morning room, overlooking the gardens of the house and the blue-green waters of the Atlantic beyond.

Crisp lemon-yellow linen, gleaming silver flatware, cut glass and bone china, all set on a circular table in the shaded curve of the windows.

Jacob began by saying how sorry he was that she'd lost her parents—even if he was thinking that she'd had no blood tie to them at all. Nevertheless, he was kind enough to express his condolences; to help her to relax and feel there was someone else, besides herself, who cared.

Her apology for not appearing again the night before was quickly dealt with.

'Dominic was right,' he assured her, gnarled fingers surprisingly dark against her creamy skin. 'I should have realised you were tired. Instead of expecting you to be as excited to see me as I was to see you.'

Cleo had no answer to that. Easy-going as he was, she hadn't to forget how she came to be here. But it wasn't as easy to hold a grudge in such beautiful surroundings. And hadn't he been as much a victim of circumstance as she was?

No!

Fortunately, her grandfather was happy to lead the conversation. He seemed quite content to describe the island and its history, entertaining her with stories of the illegal rum-running that had gone on during Prohibition in the United States.

Surprisingly, he'd also mentioned the slavery that had taken place during the late-eighteenth and early-nineteenth centuries, too. He'd shocked her by admitting that there were few families on San Clemente who could claim there was no mixed blood in their ancestry.

Indeed, she'd been so engrossed in what he was saying that it wasn't until the meal was over that Cleo realised how much about her own life he'd gleaned. Just the odd question here and there, but she'd found herself telling him about her job and about Norah, forgetting for a few moments exactly who he was.

He was a clever man, she mused, accepting his invitation to sit on the terrace for a while after breakfast. He'd probably already known half of what she'd told him. But by getting her to confide in him, he'd created a bond between them that would be that much harder to break.

'Perhaps you'd like a swim,' he remarked, apparently aware that Cleo had been eyeing the cool waters below the terrace with some envy. 'Later this afternoon, you might enjoy a walk along the shoreline. I'd like to take you myself, but for now I can recommend the pool.'

'Oh, no.' Cleo shook her head. Then, in an outright lie, 'I don't have a swimsuit, Mr Montoya.'

'If you can't call me Grandpa, call me Jacob,' he said a little tersely then, continuing his earlier suggestion. 'A swimsuit is no problem.' He gestured with his stick towards the cabanas. 'You'll find everything you need in one of the cabins. Serena always keeps a selection of swimwear for unexpected guests.'

'But I'm not really an unexpected guest, am I?' Cleo regarded him with cautious eyes. 'I think I'd rather hear why you've brought me here now. When—well, for over twenty years you've ignored my existence.'

Jacob sighed. 'It must seem that way, mustn't it?'

'It is that way,' said Cleo flatly. 'And although I appreciate that you're ill—'

'My being ill is the least of it!' exclaimed her grandfather fiercely. 'Is that what they told you? That because I'm dying I've had a change of heart?'

Cleo felt a little nervous now. She didn't want to upset him, goodness knew.

'And—and isn't that true?' she ventured, aware that she was treading into deep water. But she had a right to know, she told herself. She'd spent too many years in the dark.

The old man's fingers massaged the head of his cane for a few pregnant moments, and then he said, 'How much has Dominic told you?'

'Oh…' Cleo could feel her body getting hot now and she shifted a little uncomfortably beneath his knowing eyes. 'Well, he told me that—that Celeste—'

'Your mother.'

'All right, my mother—used to work for the Montoyas.'

'Yes, she did. She worked for Robert and Lily. I believe Dominic was very fond of her. But he was only a young boy at the time.'

'Dominic knew her?'

'Of course. She lived with the family. And until—well, until my son took a fancy to her, Lily and Celeste were good friends.'

'Friends!'

Cleo was scornful, but Jacob only shook his head. 'Yes, friends,' he insisted. 'We have no class system here on the island, Cleo. Your mother worked for my son and his wife, this is true, but she was never regarded as one of the servants.'

'So what happened?'

'You know what happened.' Jacob grimaced. 'Robert fell in love with her. Oh, yes.' He held up a hand as Cleo would have interrupted him. 'Robert did love Celeste. I am assured of that. But he loved his wife as well and he knew that their relationship would destroy Lily if she found out.'

Cleo bent her head. 'How convenient that Celeste died.'

Jacob made a sound of resignation. 'I suppose it does seem that way to you. And I accept the fact that your growing up on the island would have been a constant threat.'

'To your son!'

'And to Lily,' Jacob agreed heavily. 'She couldn't have children, you know. If she could, things might have been different.'

'I don't think so.'

Cleo couldn't help the faintly bitter edge that had entered her voice now, and Jacob stretched out a hand and gripped her arm.

'No one knows what might have happened if circumstances had been different,' he said, holding her troubled gaze with his. 'I'm not totally convinced Robert would have let you go to England. But after Celeste's death, he was a changed man.'

Cleo made a helpless gesture. 'And where did my—the Novaks fit into the equation?'

'Well…'

Jacob released her arm and lay back in his chair. He was looking very pale and Cleo realised this must be a terrible strain on him. She half wished someone—even Lily—would interrupt them. But the breeze was all that stirred the feathery palms.

'Henry was a decent man,' her grandfather said at last. 'But he was ambitious. He thought that moving to England would help him achieve the success he was striving for. He and Lucille had no children, and Lucille and Celeste had been friends. It wasn't too difficult to persuade them to adopt her daughter.'

Cleo caught her breath. Her mother—her adoptive mother—and her real mother had been friends! That at least accounted for the faded photograph she'd found among her parents' papers, after they were dead.

She frowned now. 'But it must have been a drain on their resources. I mean, my father—Henry, that is—didn't have a job to go to, did he?'

'No.' Jacob moistened his lips. 'We—Robert and I—oiled the wheels of the removal for him. It was…the least we could do.'

Cleo stared at him. 'You mean, you paid him to adopt me?' She was dismayed. 'Oh God. No one told me that!'

'Don't take it so hard, my dear.' Jacob blew out a breath. 'You have to understand, the Novaks were not wealthy people.'

'Even so…'

'They looked after you, didn't they? They loved you, I'm sure. And, judging by the way you've turned out, they did a damn good job of it as well.'

Cleo shook her head, aware that her eyes burned with unshed tears. It was all too much for her to handle. First the news that she wasn't who she'd always thought she was. And now— horror of horrors—the fact that her parents had had to be paid to adopt her.

Well, they weren't her parents, of course, she reminded herself. She mustn't forget that. And it was true, they had loved her and she'd loved them. But how much of their love had been fabricated? she wondered. She would never know now.

'This has been very hard for you,' murmured her grandfather regretfully. 'And believe me, if I could have done it any other way, I would. But we, Robert and I, respected the Novaks' wishes not to contact you. They wanted you to have nothing more to do with this family, and I suppose I can't blame them for that. But when I discovered they'd been killed in that accident—'

'All bets were off,' said Cleo bitterly, and her grandfather bowed his head in mute acknowledgement.

There was silence for a while. The breeze continued to bring a blessed freshness to the air, and the water in the pool rippled invitingly.

Glancing at her grandfather, Cleo saw he'd closed his eyes and she wondered a little anxiously if he was all right. But his chest was rising and falling rhythmically, so she felt a little better. Probably, he'd just fallen asleep.

She wished she'd agreed to take a swim now. The idea of

submerging herself in the cool water was just as attractive as it had been before.

But she was glad they had had this conversation. At least she knew now why the Novaks had adopted her. Even if she felt as if the world as she'd known it had been destroyed.

Pushing herself to her feet, she walked to the edge of the terrace and stood looking down at the marble dolphin that continuously spouted water into the pool. She wished she could be as unfeeling as the fountain. But she was far too emotional for that.

'Why don't you?' her grandfather's voice interrupted her reverie. 'Have that swim?' he suggested, and she turned to gaze at him with incredulous eyes.

'How did you know—?'

'What you were thinking?' His lined face creased into a grin. 'We're family, remember?'

Cleo shook her head. 'I think you're just very intuitive,' she said.

'Well, whatever I am, why don't you take me at my word?' He nodded towards the cabanas. 'Humour me, Cleo. I'd love to watch my beautiful granddaughter enjoying herself at last.'

Cleo had her doubts, but the temptation was greater. Besides, she suspected Jacob would relax if she proved she hadn't taken offence over what he'd told her.

And, after all, she'd wanted to know the truth, hadn't she? She'd asked him to tell her how she'd come to be living with—with the Novaks. Not the other way about.

The cabana smelled of pine and salt water. Although it was a freshwater pool, she guessed the cabins were used by anyone who wanted to change. As Jacob had said, there was a fitted rail with a row of colourful swimsuits. Tank suits and bikinis, but not a one-piece outfit in sight.

Blowing out a breath, she examined the suits rather disappointedly. But short of abandoning the idea, she would have to choose one of them to wear.

And, after all, there was no one about—well, except Lily.

But she couldn't see Dominic's mother caring to watch her take a swim.

She emerged from the cabana wearing the plainest tank suit in the collection. It was a deep blue, with white piping highlighting every seam and hem.

It left a narrow wedge of skin exposed at her midriff, but that didn't worry her. She was used to that after wearing cropped T-shirts at home.

However, the high-sided briefs made her wonder with unwilling humour if she should have taken Norah's advice and had a Brazilian wax before taking off her clothes.

Still, it was too late now. She left the cabana, pulling the elastic band off her hair and folding her hair in half before securing it again.

With her arms upraised, her breasts were lifted and the skimpy briefs threatened to reveal more than they concealed. And it was at that precise moment she saw Dominic, across the pool, standing beside her grandfather's chair.

CHAPTER SEVEN

THE breath whooshed out of her lungs with a rush. Her body suffused with heat, yet goose pimples pebbled all over her skin.

She wanted to pull her arms down, to draw the cuffs of her briefs over her buttocks. To somehow compose herself so that he wouldn't see how his appearance had affected her.

But for some reason, her limbs were frozen like a statue. And she thought how ironic it was that only minutes before she'd been imagining how unfeeling the marble dolphin was.

She wasn't unfeeling; she was hot and unsteady. Her only consolation was that surely he couldn't see the pointed hardness of her breasts outlined against the blue silk of her top.

Dominic, meanwhile, looked cool and indifferent. He was wearing another suit, although there was no formal vest or waistcoat in sight. Just Italian silk and pale grey cotton, his tie a splash of charcoal against his shirt.

She could always slip into the pool, Cleo thought, managing to bring her hands down at last, feeling the slick of moisture in her palms.

But that would be a rude and cowardly gesture. And she had no intention of proving Lily's opinion was right.

Dominic meanwhile was wishing he'd never stepped onto the terrace. He'd seen his grandfather sitting there, alone, and he'd assumed Cleo had gone back to her room. All he'd intended was to clear the air with the old man before leaving.

But now his eyes were riveted on the young woman who'd just emerged from the cabana.

God, she was beautiful, he thought. But there was something more than beauty alone that drew him to her. Sarah was beautiful, but he had never felt this way in her presence. Never felt his stomach clenching with awareness, or the wild rush of blood to his groin.

She had a sexual appeal that was beyond anything he had experienced before. And he couldn't help comparing his feelings to the feelings his adoptive father had had for her mother.

He could almost scent her, he mused grimly, even while he rejected the notion. She made him feel like some kind of jungle predator, his senses spinning with the thought of her naked in his arms.

Dammit!

'Is something wrong?'

The old man was far too perceptive, and Dominic had to physically force a hollow smile to his lips.

'I didn't realise Cleo was here,' he said, aware that his answer begged even more questions. He pushed his fists into his jacket pockets. 'Well, as you're in such good hands, I'll be on my way.'

'It's a pity you can't stay,' remarked his grandfather sagely. 'I know how much you like a swim in the pool.'

'I had one earlier,' said Dominic shortly, not best-pleased at being reminded. The brief glimpse of Cleo he'd seen on her balcony was still far too dominant in his mind.

With her hair tumbled about her shoulders, she'd drawn his eyes instinctively. In her skimpy bra and panties, she'd looked even more seductive than she did now.

'Oh, well…'

Dominic was fairly sure the old man wasn't deceived, but he wasn't about to stay around to find out.

'I'll see you tomorrow,' he said. 'You know I'm having

dinner with Sarah this evening. She was pretty peeved when I didn't get over to see her last night.'

'She'll get over it.' Jacob spoke absently, lifting a hand to Cleo as he spoke. 'Just so long as you remember we're having a special dinner here tomorrow evening. I want to introduce Cleo to our friends and neighbours. I want them to know how proud of her I am.'

Dominic stifled a sigh. 'OK.'

'Oh, and by the way…' Jacob looked up at him now '…I never thanked you for bringing my granddaughter to me, Dom. You've no idea how much it means to me to have her here.'

Dominic pulled a wry face. 'I have a pretty good idea,' he said, squeezing his grandfather's shoulder with genuine affection. 'Look after yourself, old man. And don't be overdoing things to try and impress her, yeah?'

'Then you're going to have to spend a little time with her yourself, Dom,' said Jacob staunchly. 'Introduce her to your friends. I'd like for you all to get along.'

Yeah, right.

Dominic didn't voice the words, but he wasn't deceived by the old man's suggestion. Jacob knew Sarah for one would be as keen to make a friend of Cleo as his mother.

Dominic prepared for the celebratory dinner at Magnolia Hill with little enthusiasm.

He was in no hurry to spend an evening refereeing a slanging match between his grandfather and his mother. And, judging from what Lily had said when he'd spoken to her on the phone earlier, her opinion of their unexpected guest hadn't improved with time.

He was less sure of Serena.

According to his mother, his aunt was playing a waiting game, neither applauding Cleo's arrival, nor making any attempt to alienate the girl.

Which was Serena all over, thought Dominic wryly, sliding his arms into the sleeves of a dark blue silk shirt. She must know that her position as her father's hostess could be in jeopardy and she'd be holding her cards very close to her chest.

As for Cleo herself…

Dominic buttoned his shirt with impatient fingers, studying his reflection in his dressing-room mirror without liking. He really didn't want to see her again. Not with the image of her as he'd last seen her, beside the pool, still tormenting his mind.

Of course, he'd had a valid excuse for not calling to see his grandfather the night before. The old man had known he was having dinner with Sarah, so Dominic had contented himself with a phone call instead.

Not that his dinner with Sarah had been a particularly enjoyable occasion. She'd still been brooding about his absence the previous evening, and Dominic was beginning to think their affair had run its course. Her mood had soured their meeting, and he'd been glad to get back to his own house.

He'd known Sarah had expected him to stay over. But even after she'd thrown off her petulance, he'd had enough. He doubted he could have sustained a convincing conversation. And as for going to bed with her…

Dominic closed his eyes for a moment. Then, zipping up his trousers, he emerged into the bedroom.

Sarah was standing in the middle of the floor. She had evidently been debating the merits of surprising him in either his bathroom or his dressing room, and her face fell when she saw he was fully dressed.

Dominic had half forgotten he'd invited her to the dinner party. When he'd first arrived at her house the night before, it had seemed the natural thing to do. Now, though, he was definitely regretting it…

'You're ready,' she said disappointedly, and Dominic was inordinately relieved he hadn't spent any more time than was necessary in the shower.

'What did you expect?' he asked, coming to bestow a light kiss on her expectant mouth. 'We have to be there in twenty minutes.'

'There's no rush.' Sarah's lips pouted.

'There is,' said Dominic flatly, stepping past her to pick up his cellphone from the low table beside the king-size bed. 'I promised Grandpa I wouldn't be late.'

'Oh, Grandpa!'

Sarah spoke contemptuously, and Dominic couldn't help noticing how her lips thinned when she was agitated.

Even in her apricot sequinned mini-dress, that exposed her slim legs to advantage, and with her cap of blonde hair curling confidingly under her chin, her face had a sulky arrogance that detracted somewhat from its pale beauty.

'Yes, Grandpa,' agreed Dominic, not prepared to argue. He glanced towards her. 'I assume Nelson is waiting outside. Why don't you go ahead? I've got a couple of calls to make before I leave.'

'But you're coming with me, aren't you?'

Sarah was indignant, and Dominic ran a weary hand round the back of his neck.

'I thought I'd drive my own car,' he said, aware that he was behaving badly. But, dammit, if he allowed the Cordys' chauffeur to drive them, Sarah would expect to spend the night at Turtle Cove when they got back.

So what was wrong with that?

Everything!

Sarah got the message, as he'd known she would.

'You're still sulking,' she said accusingly. 'Just because I was a bit short with you last night—not without good reason, mind you—you've decided to punish me in return.'

'Don't be ridiculous!'

Dominic wanted to laugh out loud at the ludicrousness of that statement.

'I just think it would be easier if I didn't have to rely on Nelson,' he said. 'Grandpa may decide he wants a post-mortem after the party is over. It will save you hanging around when I don't know when I'll be ready to leave.'

Sarah pursed her lips. 'Why can't Jacob wait until tomorrow

if he needs to discuss anything with you? For heaven's sake, Dom, you're in charge of the Montoya interests, not him.'

'Don't let Grandpa hear you saying that,' remarked Dominic, trying to lighten the mood. 'Anyway, it's a good idea, isn't it? And I am still pretty jet-lagged, you know.'

Sarah considered for a moment, and then came to rest her head against his shoulder. 'I'm a bitch, aren't I?'

'No.' Dominic's conscience couldn't allow her to think that. 'Look—we can spend time together when I'm not so committed,' he said, not altogether truthfully. He put an arm about her shoulders and gave her a hug. 'Right now, things are a bit…hectic. I'm sorry.'

'You mean because that girl is here,' said Sarah peevishly. 'I don't know what your grandfather's thinking of, bringing your father's bastard daughter to Magnolia Hill.'

Dominic's jaw hardened. 'I wish you wouldn't talk about her like that, Sarah,' he said coldly. 'You sound just like my mother. You can't hold Cleo responsible for what her father and mother did before she was born.'

Sarah's lips curled. 'But can you understand why—with a sweet wife like Lily—your father could risk impregnating a woman like Celeste Dubois? I mean—it's disgusting!'

'Yeah, well…'

Unfortunately, Dominic could understand his father's situation exactly.

But that was something he had no intention of acting on, so they weren't that alike, after all.

Cleo was standing beside her grandfather's chair when she saw Dominic come out of the house with a slim blonde young woman clinging to his arm.

It was evening, and beyond the candle-lit beauty of the terrace it was already pitch-dark. Only the muted roar of the sea reminded her of the walk she'd taken earlier, the perfumed scents of the flowers overlaid by the expensive fragrances worn by their female guests.

Cleo was already tired of keeping a smile plastered to her lips. Her grandfather—and Serena—had introduced her to so many people that she'd had no hope of remembering all their names.

She did know they were here for two reasons, however. One, to please her grandfather; and two, to get a look at Robert Montoya's bastard.

Ever since her grandfather's guests started arriving, she'd been aware of their interest and speculation. Aware, too, that many of the whispered conversations, taking place behind discreetly raised glasses, concerned her and her likeness not just to her mother, but to her father, as well.

Not that anyone had mentioned it to her. They'd all been very cordial, very polite. Though she couldn't exactly call them friendly.

Which was probably due to the fact that Dominic's mother had stood glaring at her all evening, making her attitude towards her father-in-law's behaviour all too obvious.

'At last,' she heard her grandfather mutter now, and guessed Dominic's late arrival was what he meant. 'Where the devil has he been?' he demanded of no one in particular. 'I told him I wanted him to be here to welcome our guests.'

Cleo thought she had an idea why his grandson's arrival had been delayed. The way the young woman with him was hanging on his arm was a fair indication, and she was sure they'd shared more than a car ride here.

Whatever, it was nothing to do with her, she assured herself fiercely. She'd be going back to England before too long and then she'd never see any of them again.

Not surprisingly, Dominic made a beeline for his grandfather, only stopping briefly along the way when one or other of Jacob's guests spoke to him.

With an easy confidence Cleo could only envy, he parried all their greetings with a rueful aside or a laughing retort, leaving an admiring group of men as well as women in his wake.

Sarah, who'd been forced to let go of his arm, followed him across the terrace. In a strapless, sequin-studded mini-dress, that suited her petite figure, she was every bit as glamorous as Cleo had anticipated Dominic's girlfriend would be.

Certainly, her outfit was far more expensive than the simple jade slip dress Cleo was wearing; her skin with that delicate look of porcelain, that made Cleo's skin look almost dusky.

'Hey, Grandpa!' Dominic exclaimed when he reached them, squatting down beside the old man's chair, his expression rueful. 'I guess I'm in the doghouse, yeah?'

Jacob gave an impatient shake of his head. 'That depends what you've got to say for yourself,' he declared drily. 'Where the hell have you been?'

'Sarah's car broke down,' Dominic replied without hesitation, and Cleo felt her own jaw drop at the total incredulity of his excuse.

'Say what?' Jacob stared at him. 'Can't you do better than that, boy?'

'It's true,' said Dominic, glancing up into Cleo's doubtful face.

Obviously she didn't believe him either, he thought, wishing it didn't matter to him. Then, straightening, he turned to Sarah, 'Do you want to tell them or shall I?'

'Oh…' Sarah pouted prettily, and Cleo wondered it if was possible to hate someone when you'd never even been introduced to them. 'Well, Nelson—that's my father's chauffeur, Mr Montoya—'

'Yes, I know who Nelson Buffett is,' Jacob interrupted her shortly, and with a little sigh she went on.

'Well, Nelson thought Daddy had put gas in the car and Daddy thought Nelson had.' She spread her hands innocently. 'It turns out, neither of them had.'

'So you ran out of gas?'

'Yes.'

Sarah nodded, her eyes drifting irresistibly to Cleo, and

Dominic realised he was being damnably ignorant in not introducing them.

But he was loath to do it. Cleo looked so beautiful this evening, and he was unwilling to give Sarah a chance to hurt her feelings as his mother had done.

Instead, he turned back to his grandfather. 'Hey, it was lucky we weren't travelling together,' he said, and saw the way Cleo's eyes widened again. 'I came along about ten minutes later in the SUV and I offered to go and get some gas for them.'

Jacob sniffed. 'And couldn't young Buffett have phoned the garage and had them bail him out?' he asked, and once again Sarah joined in.

'He did ring the garage in San Clemente, Mr Montoya, but there's nobody there at this time of the evening. And we couldn't leave poor Nelson to walk home, could we?'

Jacob grimaced. 'I suppose not,' he said grudgingly. He looked up at Cleo. 'I guess we're going to have to forgive him, eh, my dear? Oh, and by the way, you haven't met Dominic's girlfriend, have you?' He paused. 'This is Sarah, Cleo. Why don't you ask her what she'd like to drink?'

Sarah's polite words belied the flush of irritation that stained her cheeks. 'I've been here often enough to get my own drink, thank you. Or Dom can get it, can't you, darling?' She linked her arm with his again. 'How do you do—er—Cleo? Are you enjoying your stay at Magnolia Hill?'

'Very much,' Cleo was beginning, when her grandfather caught her hand in both of his.

'We're hoping she might consider making her home on San Clemente,' he said, in a voice that carried right across the terrace. 'Isn't that right, Dom? You're all for it, aren't you?'

The old devil!

Dominic's teeth ground together for a moment. The old man knew he'd never discussed any such thing, despite his suspicions of what Jacob had in mind.

But before he could make any response, Cleo said awkwardly, 'I don't think we've ever talked about that—er—Jacob.'

She refused to call him 'Grandfather' in front of all these people, even if that was the way she was beginning to think of him. 'I certainly don't think this is the time or the place—'

'Nonsense!' But Jacob seemed to realise he'd embarrassed her and he patted her hand reassuringly. 'We'll leave it for now.' He glanced round. 'Now where's Luella with the canapés? I told her I wanted them serving as soon as all the guests had arrived.'

There was a significant relaxing of the atmosphere as Jacob got determinedly to his feet. Refusing the help of either his grandson or his granddaughter, he stomped off towards the buffet tables that were set up beneath a sheltering canopy.

Catching Cleo's eye, Dominic realised that she was more upset by what had happened than either himself or Sarah. He was used to his grandfather's blunt way of speaking, but Cleo wasn't, and, detaching himself from Sarah's clinging hands, he said, 'Come on. I'll get us all a drink.' He nodded towards Cleo's glass. 'Is that a pina colada?'

'This?' Cleo was taken aback. 'Um—no. It's just pineapple juice,' she said, aware of Sarah's displeasure at this turn of events. 'And I don't need another drink, thank you.'

'Well, I do,' said Dominic flatly. And before he'd given any thought to his actions, he'd gripped Cleo's elbow with a decisive hand and turned her towards the bar set up beside the swimming pool.

He regretted it instantly. He hadn't forgotten how soft her skin was, or erased the memory of her scent, that tonight was a mixture of musk and spice and some tropical fragrance. But he had blanked it from his mind.

Now, however, it was back, more potent than before.

The side of her breast was so warm and sexy against his suddenly moist fingers. And if she was wearing a bra, it was doing little to hide the way her nipples had peaked and were pressing unrestrainedly against the thin fabric of her dress.

Oh, God!

His arousal was as painful as it was inappropriate. With

Sarah—the girl he'd brought to the party, dammit—following closely behind, he had no right to be feeling as if the ground was shifting beneath his feet.

Yet it was. And, heaven knew, he wanted to touch Cleo. Not as he was touching her now, but privately, intimately. To bury his hands in her silky hair and bury another part of his body— that was hot and hard and pulsing with life—in some place equally soft, but tight and wet as well.

He wondered if she'd heard his hoarse intake of breath, the surely audible pounding of his heart. She must have felt his fingers tightening almost involuntarily, because she turned to look at him, her eyes almost as wide and elemental as his own.

He abruptly let her go, surging ahead to where a handful of waiters tended the comprehensive array of drinks his grandfather had provided.

'Scotch,' he said without hesitation. 'No. No ice. Just as it is.' Then he raised the single malt to his lips and swallowed half of it before turning to address the two girls.

Cleo was wishing she'd accompanied her grandfather, after all. She was far too aware of Dominic, far too conscious of the fact that in other circumstances she wouldn't have wanted him to let her go.

Everything about him disturbed her: from the lean, muscular strength of his body to the intensely masculine perfume of his skin.

When he'd taken her arm, his heat had surrounded her. The hardness of his fingers gripping her arm had felt almost possessive. She'd wanted to rub herself against him, like a cat that was wholly sensitive to his touch.

She still felt that way, she thought unsteadily, and then had to compose herself when Sarah caught her gaze. Was the other woman aware that Dominic was a fallen angel? That beneath his enigmatic exterior beat the heart of a rogue male?

'How long do you expect to stay on the island?'

Sarah got straight to the point and Cleo told herself she was grateful.

'I— Just a few more days,' she said, aware that she'd lowered her voice in the hope that Dominic wouldn't hear her.

'Oh…' Sarah looked slightly taken aback. But pleased, Cleo thought. Perhaps she'd expected a more aggressive kind of response.

Though why should she? She and Dominic had looked very much a couple when they'd arrived tonight.

'So you're not planning on making your home here?'

Sarah was persistent, and Cleo wished she could just leave her and Dominic to sort out their own problems.

'Not at the moment,' she replied at last, not wanting to say anything to offend her grandfather. But she was grateful when someone else attracted Sarah's attention.

She didn't really dislike the girl, she assured herself. It was just that they had nothing in common.

Except Dominic…

'Here!'

She was forced to look at him again when Dominic took her drink from her and thrust another glass into her hand.

'What is this?' she protested, managing to instil a convincing edge of indignation in her voice. 'I said I didn't want another drink.' She sniffed suspiciously. 'Ugh—this is alcoholic!'

'Damn right,' agreed Dominic, finishing his own drink and turning to ask the waiter for a refill. 'This is supposed to be a celebration. You can't celebrate with a pineapple juice and soda.'

'Who says?' Cleo leant past him to replace the glass on the table that was serving as a bar, intensely aware of him beside her. She cast a nervous glance behind her. 'I wonder where your grandfather is. I think I ought to go and find him.'

Dominic sucked in a breath. Her bare arm had brushed along his midriff as she deposited the glass and he felt as if someone had scorched him with a burning knife.

'Don't,' he said barely audibly, his voice rough with emotion. 'The old man knows what he's doing.' He blew out a tortured breath that seared along her hairline. 'God knows, I wish I did.'

Startled eyes lifted to his, liquid dark eyes that Dominic felt he could have happily drowned in.

'I—I don't know what you mean,' she said, a catch in her breathing, and his hard-on threatened to drag him to his knees.

You do, his eyes accused her. But then Sarah was beside them, and Cleo hurriedly made good her escape.

CHAPTER EIGHT

CLEO walked along the shoreline in the coolness of early morning.

It was barely light and, apart from a few seabirds, she was alone on the beach.

All the guests had left in the early hours. They'd stayed much longer than she'd expected, particularly as her grandfather had retired soon after midnight.

In his absence, Serena had done her best to provide entertainment for their guests. Earlier in the evening, a group of West Indian musicians had arrived, and although Cleo had anticipated a lot of noisy percussion, she couldn't have been more wrong.

These musicians used their steel drums to produce melodic liquid sounds that played on the senses as well as the mind. Rippling chords of magic that filled any awkward silences with rhythm and enchantment.

The area around the pool had been cleared and there'd been some dancing. But, even though Cleo had danced with a couple of Jacob's friends, she'd avoided the younger men like the plague.

The last thing she needed was for these people—who probably neither liked her nor trusted her—to get the idea that she was like her mother. She didn't know much about Celeste, of course. Only what her grandfather had told her. But nothing could alter the fact that she'd had an affair with a married man.

Her employer, no less.

She supposed, from the Montoyas' point of view, the evening had been a success. She'd been introduced to San Clemente society, and Jacob's intentions towards her had been made plain for all to see.

But they were wrong.

There'd been a subtle change in the atmosphere after her grandfather had retired. No one had been rude, but their questions about her life in England had seemed more pointed somehow. She'd got the feeling they regarded her with a mixture of curiosity and blame.

But it wasn't her fault that her father had seduced her mother, she told herself fiercely. And if they had fallen in love...

She had made sure she'd kept out of Dominic's way. And with Sarah constantly at his side, it hadn't been too difficult. Besides, with talk of a possible wedding on everyone's lips, she'd had little to contribute.

She'd wondered a couple of times if Sarah was speaking more loudly for her benefit. She was obviously suspicious of Cleo, and she and Dominic's mother seemed to have a lot in common.

Whatever, Cleo had been glad to leave the party herself at about 2 a.m. She hadn't been tired, exactly, but she'd definitely had enough of being treated like the skeleton at the feast.

Now it was a little before six, and she'd left the house with a feeling of deliverance. She'd wanted to get away; not just from Magnolia Hill, but from her thoughts.

The tide was coming in. The cool water brushed against her toes, and Cleo kicked off her sandals and allowed the waves to swirl about her feet.

She'd been mad to come down to the beach in high-heeled wedges anyway. But then, she was still wearing the dress she'd worn the evening before. Having spent the last three hours lying sleepless on her bed, it had seemed like too much trouble to change.

She'd stopped to examine the pearly spiral of a conch shell when she felt the distinct vibration of footsteps on the sand.

Lifting her head, she saw a man approaching, his profile still indistinct in the morning half-light. He was some distance away, but he was running in her direction. Long legs pumping rhythmically, arms swinging to match his muscular pace.

It looked like Dominic, but it couldn't be him. He had brought Sarah to the party. It was a cinch he'd taken her home. To his home, if she was any judge of the other girl's intentions, thought Cleo ruefully. There was no way he'd have stayed at Magnolia Hill.

But it was Dominic!

As he drew nearer, Cleo recognised his height and his muscular build. Broad shoulders, narrow hips and a tight butt, she conceded reluctantly. Outlined to perfection in black Lycra shorts.

He obviously enjoyed running, judging by the damp patches on his black cotton vest, and the streams of perspiration running down his chest. Despite the fact that she'd had no sleep, her adrenalin kicked up another notch.

'Hi.' Dominic slowed as he reached her, his eyes taking in the fact that she hadn't changed from what she'd been wearing the night before. 'Going somewhere special?'

Cleo's chin jutted. She wouldn't allow him to make fun of her. 'I haven't been to bed,' she said, as if that wasn't already obvious. 'I'm sorry. Is that a problem for you?'

Privately Dominic thought it was one hell of a problem, judging from the way he reacted to her. But after last evening's fiasco, he was determined to keep things simple.

'Not for me,' he said, bending forward and bracing himself with his hands on his knees to avoid looking at her. He was uncomfortably aware that his quickened heartbeat was as much mentally as physically induced.

But eventually, he had to straighten. 'So,' he said evenly, 'did you enjoy the party? I seem to remember the guest of honour disappeared.'

Cleo forced herself to look at the horizon. The faintest trace of pink was brushing the ocean and she pretended an interest in the view. 'I wasn't the guest of honour,' she said tensely. 'Or if I was, your guests didn't know it.'

Dominic scowled. 'What's that supposed to mean? What did they say to you?'

'Oh—nothing.'

Cleo wished she hadn't started this. Not when he was standing so close that the heat of his body enveloped her in its spell. She could smell his sweat; smell *him*; and her mouth was suddenly as dry as parchment. Even her legs felt unsteady as she met his accusing gaze.

'Forget it,' she said, trying to behave naturally. 'Why aren't you at—what was it you called your house—Pelican Bay?' She paused, and then added brightly, 'Did Sarah stay over as well?'

Dominic ignored her question. 'I want to know what's upset you,' he said. 'Did my mother say something? Did Sarah?'

'Heavens, no.' Cleo spread her hands, not allowing herself to look at him again. 'But, let's face it, your guests didn't just come to be polite. They were—curious. About me.'

Dominic stifled a groan. 'They were curious, sure—'

'I rest my case.' Cleo permitted herself another brief glance in his direction. 'Curious—and suspicious. They think I want Jacob's money!' She made a sound of disgust. 'If they only knew!'

'Only knew what?'

Dominic's hand reached for her bare arm and instantly her skin felt as if he'd burned her. The pain that flared in the pit of her stomach was purely sexual, its fiery tendrils spreading down both her legs.

She knew an urgent need to press herself against him, to allow the fever smouldering inside her to take control. But no matter how sorry he was, how sympathetic, he could do nothing physically to ease her pain.

'It doesn't matter,' she said, stepping back from him,

breaking his hold, and Dominic raked frustrated fingers though his hair.

But it was just as well one of them had some sense, he conceded, even if he could have done without her conscience asserting itself right now.

He felt the ache between his legs, glanced down and saw the unmistakable swell of his erection. What did this woman do to him? he wondered. One touch and his body took control.

'I think you're exaggerating people's reactions,' he said harshly, in an effort to ground himself. But even to his own ears, his voice was edged with strain.

'Well, I don't want your grandfather's money,' she said. 'So tell that to whoever's prepared to listen. I'll be leaving here in a few days anyway. Then it won't matter either way.'

Dominic stared at her with anguished eyes. Dammit, he didn't want to see her go. But to tell her that would be madness. He wasn't interested in making that kind of commitment, to her or anyone else.

He had to put any thought of a relationship between them out of his mind...

With a muffled oath, he abandoned any attempt to reason with her. Turning, he plunged into the water, hoping against hope that the ocean would ease his mangled emotions.

Cleo's lips parted in astonishment when she saw what he was doing. Dominic had gone into the water still wearing his vest and shorts. Was he mad or simply reckless? Why did it matter so much what he did?

She stared after him, watching as he struck out strongly into the current. The weight of his clothes didn't appear to hamper his progress, but she was anxious just the same.

Allowing herself to tread a little deeper into the shallows, she wished she had the nerve to do something reckless. And as the salty water swirled about her ankles, she could feel the erratic beating of her heart.

Dominic had almost disappeared. His head appeared only

fleetingly above the waves. She prayed he knew what he was doing. That he had the sense to know when to turn back.

A thin line of gold was fringing the horizon now, and in the growing light she saw—much to her relief—that he was swimming back to shore. She envied him his skill, the strength with which his arms attacked the waves and defeated them. He looked like a dark, powerful predator moving through the water, and she knew if she had any sense she'd be long gone before he reached the beach.

But still she waited.

Dominic reached the shallows and, pushing himself to his feet, he walked towards her. He was dripping water everywhere, from his hair, from his arms, from his legs. Even from his lashes as he blinked to clear his gaze.

Pushing his hair back with both hands, he caught Cleo's gaze and held it. He knew she'd been watching him, had felt her staring at him, even with so many yards of ocean between them. And, as her eyes dropped down his body, he realised his swim had done nothing to kill his lust.

With a feeling of inevitability, he closed the gap between them. Then, before she could do anything to stop him, he reached out and jerked her into his arms.

His mouth found hers and it was just as sweet and lush and hot as he had imagined. His tongue licked, probed, seeking and finding entry. And she opened to him eagerly, it seemed, welcoming his invasion.

Cleo's world spun. To try and steady herself, she clutched his hips above the cropped waistband of his shorts. And found smooth muscled flesh, narrow bones that moved beneath her fingers. Raw, uncontrolled passion in the way his body ground against hers.

'Cleo!'

She heard his strangled groan as if from a distance. But whatever protest it might have signalled made little difference to his urgent assault on her emotions.

His tongue mated with hers, velvet-soft and undeniably

sexual. Cleo felt as if she was drowning in sensation, the will to keep a hold on her senses as fleeting as the clouds that briefly veiled the sun.

Dominic deepened the kiss, his hands slipping the narrow straps of her dress off her shoulders. He seemed to delight in the silky smoothness of her olive-toned skin.

As the thin fabric dropped away, Cleo made a futile attempt to stop it. Drawing back from his kiss, she gazed at him wildly, her breathing as uneven as her pounding heartbeat.

'Let me,' Dominic insisted, removing her fingers. And, as the dress fell to her waist, he cupped her breasts in his eager hands.

His thumbs rubbed abrasively over the tender dusky nipples. They were already tight, he saw, and swollen with need. Then, dropping onto his knees in front of her, he let the dress fall about her ankles. He apparently didn't care that it was now as wet as he was. Instead, he buried his face against her quivering mound.

Cleo's legs shook. Try as she might, she couldn't seem to think coherently, let alone push him away. She was naked, but for the lacy thong that Norah had assured her was all she needed under the flimsy chiffon. And when Dominic licked her navel, she let out a trembling cry.

Dominic's body felt as if it was on fire. As he pressed his face against her softness, his lungs quickly filled with her exotic scent. She was satin and silk, the rarest of spices, and oh, so responsive. His hands gripped the backs of her thighs. He wanted to rip the scrap of lace away.

It barely did the job anyway, he acknowledged. Dark curls spilled out at either side, and he wondered if those hidden lips were moist. He guessed they were, slick with the arousal rising to his nostrils. His hands moved to cup her rounded bottom. Just touching her like this was both a heaven and a hell.

He wanted to touch her everywhere, he wanted to touch her and taste her, and spread those gorgeous legs so he could—

Sanity struck him like a peen hammer. They were here—on a private beach, it was true—but one of his grandfather's groundsmen raked the sand every morning. How would Cleo feel if someone saw them? While he might not have any inhibitions, Dominic was fairly sure Cleo would.

Abandoning the erotic image of laying her down on the warm sand and relieving the hard-on he'd had since he'd first seen her on the beach, Dominic got reluctantly to his feet.

Dammit, he thought, he'd been semi-aroused since their confrontation the night before. If you could call what had happened between them a confrontation. Whatever, he'd wanted her then and he wanted her now.

God help him!

Even so, he couldn't deny himself the pleasure of lifting one of her pouting breasts to his mouth and suckling briefly on its puckered tip. She tasted so good; so irresistible. How could he let her go?

Desire sparked anew, and he opened his lips wide and allowed her nipple to brush the roof of his mouth. It was all unbearably sensual, this carnal need he had to make her want him as much as he wanted her. His hands followed the sensitive hollow of her spine, arching her against him, letting her feel what she was doing to him.

The unmistakable roar of the tractor arrested him before he could drag his sodden vest over his head and gather her against him. He'd wanted to feel those button-hard nipples against his bare chest, but it was too late.

'For pity's sake, let me go!'

Dominic didn't know whether Cleo's frantic words sourced a belated resistance on her part or a sudden awareness of the tractor's approach. But they were a shocking reminder of what he was doing; or what he'd *done*.

With a feeling of remorse, he stumbled back from her. But when he would have bent to pick up her dress, she beat him to it, wrenching it away from his grasp.

Giving it only the most perfunctory of shakes, she stepped into it, hauling the straps up over her shoulders and recoiling from the damp clamminess of the skirt.

Cleo had heard the engine, but she was wondering who could be driving along the sand at this hour of the morning. Whoever it was, she should be grateful, she thought, avoiding Dominic's eyes with an urgency that bordered on paranoia.

Dear heaven, what had she been thinking of? How had she allowed such a thing to happen? After everything she'd said. How could she have been so stupid?

The dress was gritty as well as wet, its abrasive folds like sandpaper against her sensitive skin. How on earth was she going to get into the house unnoticed? She could imagine how she would feel if anyone—her mind switched instinctively to Lily—saw her.

'Cleo, dammit—'

Dominic put out a hand as she snatched up her sandals and started away from him. But she easily evaded his touch.

'Go home, Dominic,' she said, her voice as unsteady as her legs. But she couldn't blame him entirely. 'This—this never happened.'

'We both know it did,' said Dominic harshly as the tractor rolled into view. He swore then. 'Look, why don't you let me take you back to my house? We can dry your dress—'

'Yeah, right.' Cleo regarded him incredulously. 'Do you honestly think I'd go anywhere with you?'

Then, her eyes widening at the sight of the heavy vehicle, she backed away from him. Stumbling a little, she turned and hurried away towards the house.

Dominic swore again. Raking frustrated hands through his hair, he watched her disappear through the trellis gate that led into his grandfather's garden.

He hoped to God that she didn't encounter his mother. Lily Montoya was already suspicious of the girl and she wouldn't mince her words. If she discovered Cleo in that state and then learned that Dominic had been on the beach with her, she'd certainly demand an explanation.

One that he didn't have to give, admitted Dominic grimly. He had the feeling that his whole day was only going to go from bad to freaking worse.

CHAPTER NINE

'WHAT the hell did you think you were doing with my grand-daughter?'

It was later that morning.

Dominic didn't know if Cleo had made it into the house without encountering either Serena or his mother. But, evidently, nothing escaped the eagle eye of his grandfather.

Dominic himself was hardly in the mood for an argument. He'd returned to his own house to shower and change before heading for the Montoya Corporation's headquarters in San Clemente.

Then, striding into his own suite of offices, he'd informed his staff that he wasn't to be disturbed.

Not that that counted for anything when Jacob Montoya demanded to see him. He'd heard the old man giving his assistant hell even through the door of the outer office. By the time Jacob appeared, Dominic was on his feet and ready to defend himself. He thought it was typical that the old man should have chosen today to make one of his infrequent forays into town.

Dominic's PA, Hannah Gerard, a pleasant-faced woman of middle years, hovered anxiously behind the visitor.

'May I get you some coffee, Mr Montoya?' she asked, including both men in her enquiry.

However, it was Jacob who waved his stick somewhat irritably and said, 'Not now, woman. I want to talk to my grandson. We'll let you know if we want anything. Now, scoot!'

Hannah's face flushed with embarrassment and Dominic moved swiftly round the desk to take the woman's arm. 'That's OK, Hannah,' he said gently, urging her towards the door. 'As Mr Montoya says, we're good. I'll let you know if we need anything, right?'

'Yes, sir.'

Hannah was obviously relieved to return to her own office, and Dominic closed the door and leant back against it for a moment, viewing his visitor with curious eyes.

Jacob wasn't usually so brusque with his employees. Dominic's nerves tightened at the scowling expression on his grandfather's face.

'Is something wrong?'

'You tell me.'

Jacob shifted to lower himself into the armchair opposite Dominic's desk. He hooked his walking stick over the arm and then delivered his bombshell.

'What the hell did you think you were doing with my grand-daughter?'

Dominic sucked in a breath and then blew it out again on a long sigh.

There was no point in denying that he'd been with Cleo. Somehow—God knew how!—Jacob knew. Or thought he did.

He exchanged a look with the old man, wondering if someone had seen them and reported to him. What had they seen? Everything? His lower body heated at the memory. Or was Jacob just fishing because he'd found out Cleo had been soaked to the skin?

Now he pushed himself away from the door and circled his desk. Then, spreading his hands on its granite surface, he said evenly. 'What did you think I was doing?'

'Don't get clever with me, Dom. I know what you were doing. I saw you.' Jacob's lips curled triumphantly. 'You forget, I get up early in the mornings and my balcony overlooks the beach.'

Dominic stifled an inward groan.

He remembered all too clearly what they—what *he*—had been doing. Even from a distance it would have been impossible not to see that he had kissed her. And almost stripped her naked, kneeling on the sand, pressing his face into her—

'You damn near had sex with her!' exclaimed his grandfather angrily. 'Didn't you care that people might see you? Your mother, perhaps?'

Dominic shrugged and, pushing back from the desk, sank down into his own chair. 'I didn't think,' he said honestly. 'It was a mistake.' He paused. 'It won't happen again.'

'Damn right!' Jacob scowled at him with piercing blue eyes. 'I thought you had more sense. Can't you see the girl's fragile; vulnerable?'

Dominic's eyes darkened. 'You've made your point, old man. You don't have to labour it. I made a mistake and I'm sorry, OK? I'm not about to ruin her life.'

'The way your father ruined her mother's?' suggested Jacob maliciously. 'No, I won't let you do that.'

Dominic groaned. 'Look, is there any point to this? I've said I'm sorry and I am.'

His jaw tightened. Sorry his grandfather had had to be involved, anyway.

Jacob hesitated, his manner softening. 'But you like the girl, don't you? Silly question, of course you do. All that dark silky hair and smooth almond flesh. Kind of gets under your skin, doesn't she?'

Dominic's jaw dropped. 'Are you saying—?'

'That she gets under my skin?' Jacob swore impatiently. 'Get over yourself, boy. I'm not talking personally.' His scowl returned. 'I'm only saying I can see how a young buck like yourself might be smitten. She's certainly got more about her than the girls you usually bring to Magnolia Hill.'

Dominic stared at him in disbelief. 'A few minutes ago you were reminding me of my responsibilities.'

'I know, I know.' Jacob moved his stick agitatedly. 'But maybe I was too rash. Maybe you and Cleo should get together.

My grandson and my granddaughter. Yes, that is a very appeal-ing image.'

'No!'

Dominic spoke heatedly, and his grandfather regarded him with calculating eyes.

'You haven't heard what I have to say yet,' he said harshly. 'Don't go second-guessing me before I tell you what I have in mind.'

'I don't care what you have in mind,' retorted Dominic grimly. 'I was out of line this morning. I admit it. But if you think you can manipulate me as you manipulated Serena, you've got another think coming. And if you don't like it, well—tough.'

His grandfather didn't react as he'd expected however. Instead of arguing with him, a mocking smile tipped up the old man's mouth.

'OK, OK,' he said. 'If that's the way you feel, I'll say no more about it.' He reached across the desk and pressed the button for the intercom. 'Let's have that coffee, shall we? You look as if you need something to kick you into shape.'

Dominic dragged weary hands down his face, feeling the scrape of stubble he'd been too preoccupied to shave. He didn't feel as if he'd won the argument. He felt agitated and frustrated in equal measures.

When Hannah knocked timidly at the door, Jacob summoned her in. And then ordered coffee for two with the kind of charming diffidence that left the woman wondering if she'd only imagined his anger earlier.

'So,' he said, when she'd departed again, 'what are you planning on doing for the rest of the day? I had thought of bringing Cleo into town, showing her around, giving her a taste of what she's been missing all these years. What do you think?'

Dominic gnawed at his lower lip. 'What do you mean? Showing her around? You don't intend to bring her here, do you?'

'Why not?' The old man was irritatingly bland. 'You have no objections, do you?'

'No.' But Dominic's nerves tightened at the thought of seeing Cleo again. 'I—just don't think she'll want to do that, that's all.'

'Why?' Jacob was suspicious. 'What has she said to you?'

'Nothing.' Dominic blew out a resigned breath. 'Hell, old man, she doesn't talk to me.'

'No, I noticed that,' remarked his grandfather sharply, and Dominic ran damp palms over the arms of his chair. 'But I want you to know, I'm hoping to persuade Cleo to make her home on San Clemente. And I don't want you doing anything to queer my pitch.'

Dominic shook his head. 'You'll probably do that yourself,' he muttered, and the old man gave him an angry look.

'What are you talking about?'

'Oh—' Dominic wished he'd never started this '—I just don't think she's happy here.'

'She didn't enjoy the party?' Jacob could be disconcertingly astute. 'I noticed she was still wearing the dress she wore last night when I saw you two this morning. Did someone upset her? Did *you* upset her?'

Then he snorted. 'No, don't answer that. Of course you upset her. Trying to seduce her. My God, don't you have any respect for her at all?'

'Of course I do.' Dominic spoke fiercely, refusing to admit that his behaviour might have had any bearing on the way Cleo was feeling. He groaned. 'Look, you can't expect everyone you know to like her, just because you say so, old man.'

'So someone did say something to upset her last night. After I'd gone to bed, I'll wager.' He scowled. 'Go on. You might as well tell me what it was.'

Dominic sighed. 'Maybe,' he said reluctantly, 'maybe— people asked questions. They were curious about her. You can't blame them for that.'

'Can't I?'

The return of Hannah with the tray of refreshments provided a welcome break in the conversation.

Dominic thanked her and assured her he could handle it, and after she'd gone he poured them both a cup of the strong beverage.

Then, sinking down into his chair again, he allowed himself a moment's respite. But he knew his grandfather too well to imagine that the old man would leave it there.

'They blame her, don't they?' Jacob said, making no attempt to drink his coffee. 'Those idiots blame her for what her parents did.' He thumped his cane on the floor. 'Dammit, Dom, it's unreasonable. It wasn't her fault.'

'I know.' Dominic replaced his cup in its saucer. 'And, in time, people will begin to see her for the—the attractive young woman she is.'

'As you do?' Jacob was sardonic. 'Or are you like them, Dom? Was the way you treated Cleo this morning an example of how you really feel about her?'

Cleo was standing beside the pool looking down into the blue water, when her grandfather came to join her.

It was the morning after that disastrous encounter with Dominic on the beach, and she was relieved she hadn't seen him since.

The previous day, she'd had only Serena and Lily for company. Dominic had evidently left before breakfast, and when she'd ventured downstairs again it was to find she had the morning room to herself.

Not that she'd been hungry. Some orange juice, a cup of coffee and a fresh nectarine satisfied her, and she was grateful not to have to explain herself to anyone else.

Lunch had been a different affair.

Both Serena and Lily had joined her at the table, Serena taking the time to inform her that her grandfather had gone into town.

'He's gone to the office to see Dominic,' she'd said tersely, in answer to her sister-in-law's query. 'But he should be resting, Lily, not risking his health over something he can do nothing about.'

Or some*one*, Cleo had reflected uneasily, when Lily cast a speculative glance her way. But she didn't see how she could be held responsible for her grandfather's behaviour. She hadn't even spoken to him since last night.

'Jacob always was a stubborn man,' Lily had declared carelessly. 'But Dominic won't let him do anything silly. Whatever ideas may have been put into his head.'

Cleo had caught her breath at this.

'I hope you're not implying that I had anything to do with Jacob's going into town!' she'd exclaimed defensively. And even Serena had been taken aback by the fierceness of her tone.

'Why, no.'

For once, Lily had seemed at a loss for words, and Cleo pressed on.

'But you were implying that I might have had some ulterior motive for coming here, weren't you? Do you think I want Jacob's money, Mrs Montoya? Do you honestly believe that any amount of money could compensate me for everything I've lost?'

Lily had swallowed a little nervously. 'That's easy to say, Ms Novak—'

'No, it's not easy to say, Mrs Montoya.'

Cleo had had enough of being the silent victim, and although she'd been fighting back tears, she'd had to speak out.

'I was happy in England, believe it or not. Six months ago, I hadn't a care in the world.'

Well, that hadn't been precisely true. But everyone had problems, even a wealthy woman like Lily, who must have been as devastated by her husband's betrayal as Cleo herself.

'I—I had a good home,' she'd continued, a little huskily. 'A loving family; a job I like.' She paused. 'When my parents—the only parents I'd ever known—were killed, I was shattered. I didn't think anything worse could happen to me. And then—

and then Serena turned up and told me that my whole life up until that point had been a lie.'

'I'm sure Lily didn't mean to offend you, Cleo,' Serena had broken in anxiously, evidently aware of the bigger picture here. She'd known Jacob wouldn't be at all pleased if he thought the other women in his household had been upsetting his grand-daughter.

'Is that true?'

Cleo had held Dominic's mother's gaze, her own eyes dark and sparkling with unshed tears. And, with a little shrug, Lily had given a little ground.

'Perhaps I have been a little hasty in judging you, Ms Novak,' she'd conceded, tracing the rim of her plate with a purple-tipped nail. Her shoulders lifted again. 'We shall see.'

Her reluctance to admit anything had been apparent, but to avoid any further unpleasantness, Cleo had let it go. Besides, how could she sustain her animosity towards a woman who had been as innocent a victim as herself?

In any case, Serena had smoothed the waters with a comment about the lobster pâté she'd been spreading on wafer-thin biscuits. Dominic's mother had seemed equally eager to change the subject and that was that.

Not that Lily had spoken directly to Cleo throughout the rest of the meal, though she had considered her from time to time from behind the shelter of her wine glass. What had she really been thinking? Cleo had wondered. Did Lily still believe she'd wanted to come here?

The rest of the day had been something of an anticlimax. Serena had offered to take her shopping in San Clemente, but Cleo had politely refused her invitation. She was fairly sure the offer had only been made as a kind of sweetener, and she had no desire to impose her company on anyone else.

Instead, she'd spent some time by the pool before returning to her room and flaking out for a couple of hours. Her sleepless night had caught up with her, and it was nearing dinner time when she'd gone downstairs again.

Only to find there was just to be Serena and herself for the evening meal.

'My father sends his apologies,' Serena had said. 'But that trip into town has worn him out. He tries to do too much and his body betrays him.' She'd forced a smile. 'He'll be all right tomorrow.'

'You're sure?'

Cleo had found she was really concerned, and Serena had given her a reassuring look.

'Oh, yes,' she'd said. 'He wants you to join him for breakfast. Believe me, nothing will stop him from spending as much time with you as he can.'

And now, as proof of that statement, Jacob took Cleo's arm.

'Come along,' he said. 'We can talk over breakfast. I thought you might like to try Luella's maple pancakes. They're Dominic's favourites.' He gave her a calculating sideways glance. 'It's a pity he's not here.'

Cleo permitted herself a slight smile of acquiescence, but she didn't say anything. If her grandfather had known what had been going on, he might not have been so generous towards the younger man.

She contemplated for a moment what Jacob might say if she told him. But she'd never been a sneak and she wouldn't start now.

They ate in the morning room, as they had two days ago, and Cleo did her best to do justice to the pancakes Luella had supplied. They were delicious, but once again she wasn't hungry. She thought ruefully that if she stayed here long, she'd soon be as thin as Serena.

'I thought I'd take you into San Clemente today,' Jacob said, pouring himself more coffee. 'We'll have lunch with Dom. On the yacht, I think. It's time you learned a little more about the Montoya Corporation.'

'Oh…' Cleo's throat dried. The last thing she wanted to do was spend time in Dominic's company. 'Um—will your grandson's girlfriend be joining us, too?'

Jacob pulled a wry face. 'Do you mean Sarah?' he asked. 'No, I shouldn't think so. Why?' His brows ascended. 'Did you and she get along?'

Cleo bent her head over her plate. 'I only spoke to her very briefly,' she murmured, and her grandfather gave a mocking snort.

'I didn't think you two had much in common,' he said, and, glancing up, Cleo found him grinning. ''Cept maybe Dom himself, hmm? How about that?'

'What do you mean?'

The words were out before she could prevent them, and Jacob arched a sardonic brow.

'Well, you like your brother, don't you, Cleo? It seemed to me when you arrived that you'd come to depend on him, quite a lot.'

Cleo pressed her lips together. 'He's not my brother.'

'As good as.' Jacob was dismissive. 'Why's it matter, anyway? You're both my grandchildren. And when I'm gone and Serena's married, you'll be the only Montoyas left.'

Cleo's jaw dropped. 'I didn't know Serena was getting married.'

'Nor does she—yet.' The old man grimaced. 'But she and Michael Cordy—that's Lily's cousin—have been friends since they were children. And since his first wife died, he's been looking for a replacement.'

Cleo stared at him incredulously. 'But does she love him?'

'Well…' Jacob considered. 'She's turned him down a time or two in the past. Under some mistaken impression that I needed her here. But that was before he married someone else.' He chuckled. 'It's amazing how much more attractive something becomes if it's forbidden fruit.' He paused. 'I guess you know that.'

'Me?' Cleo heard the squeak in her voice and struggled to control it. 'How should I know?'

'Why—your father and your mother. What did you think I

meant?' asked Jacob innocently. 'If their relationship wasn't forbidden fruit, then I don't know what it was.'

'Oh…' Cleo swallowed a little convulsively, not totally convinced that he was being completely honest.

But he couldn't know about her and Dominic. How could he? Not unless Dominic had spilled the beans, and something told her that that was the last thing he would do.

'Anyway—how about it?' Jacob asked. 'This trip I've got planned for us? You'd like to see the town of San Clemente, wouldn't you? This island's your home, Cleo. I want you to love it just as much as I do.'

The idea of loving anything—or anybody—was not something Cleo wanted to think about at that moment. Whatever Jacob said, how could she even think of staying here? Apart from all the obvious problems, there was still Dominic. She was not going to become his mistress as her mother had become Robert's.

Now, however, she chose her words with care.

'I—I would like to see San Clemente, of course,' she said. 'But perhaps we could just drive through the town instead of stopping for lunch.' She paused. 'Serena told me you tired yourself out yesterday. I don't think it's wise to risk your health by doing too much today.'

'Rubbish!' Jacob was impatient. 'When you don't know how much time you've got left, you don't put off until tomorrow what you can do today. Believe me, my dear, I have no intention of killing myself. As I say, we'll have lunch on the yacht. You'll like that. Then I'll have a rest in one of the cabins, while Dominic gives you a tour of the town.'

Cleo stifled a moan. 'Dominic may not want—may not have time,' she amended quickly, 'to take me sightseeing.'

'He'll make time,' declared her grandfather confidently. 'He's his own boss. No one tells him what to do.'

Except you, thought Cleo unhappily, but Jacob only winked at her.

'Now, are you finished?' he asked. 'Good. Then go and get

your handbag or whatever else you need. I'll have Sam bring the car round, so don't be long.'

Cleo wanted to protest.

She wanted to say that Dominic wouldn't want to have lunch with someone for whom he evidently had so little respect.

She wanted to suggest Jacob start making arrangements for her to return to England at the end of this week instead of next.

But over all her objections, she felt an unmistakable surge of excitement.

And how ridiculous was that?

CHAPTER TEN

DOMINIC lounged in his chrome and white leather chair, one arm hooked over its back, and wished the glass he was holding contained whisky.

Wine was all very well, and his grandfather was something of a connoisseur. But Dominic needed something stronger. Something to stop his eyes from straying in Cleo's direction every chance they had.

He'd tried to concentrate on his surroundings. They were having lunch on the sundeck of the company's yacht, shaded from too much brilliance by a huge canopy, and it was certainly a spectacular setting.

The little town of San Clemente climbed the hill behind the marina, colour-washed walls and red-tiled roofs providing a stunning backdrop to the blue, blue water.

A breeze blew up off the water, rattling the ties of the other yachts moored in the adjoining slips. It lifted the fringe of the canopy; caused a silky coil of Cleo's hair to curl about her shoulder.

Dammit!

The trouble was, she looked so bloody attractive. She was wearing an off-the-shoulder top of some bronze-coloured fabric that hugged her breasts and outlined her hips. Knee-length shorts exposed bare calves and narrow ankles. She wore a gold chain round her ankle, drawn to his attention by provocative four-inch heels.

There were huge gold rings in her ears, too, that brushed her bare shoulders every time she moved her head. Her hair was drawn loosely back from her face and tied at her nape with a chiffon scarf. But that didn't stop errant strands escaping and causing him no end of grief.

He swallowed the remainder of the wine in his glass and reached for the bottle of Merlot as his grandfather spoke.

'Isn't this nice?' the old man said, including both of them in his sharp appraisal. 'My two grandchildren and myself, having lunch together. What could be nicer, eh, Dom?'

'Indeed,' Dominic said drily, refilling his wine glass with a surprisingly steady hand. Considering the rest of his body was taut with frustration, he thought he managed it very well. 'What could be nicer?'

Cleo cast a wary look in his direction. She had few doubts that Dominic wasn't enjoying the meal. From the moment they'd arrived at the Montoya Corporation's offices, she'd sensed his resistance to the outing. If there'd been any way he could have got out of joining them without offending his grandfather, she was sure he would have done so.

But, apart from the respect Dominic evidently had for the old man, Jacob was seriously ill, and his time was limited. It would have taken a more ruthless man than Dominic to deny such a simple request.

'I hope you're not drinking too much, boy.' Jacob was nothing if not direct. He nodded to Dominic's plate, where the better part of his risotto was congealing in the heat. 'You've hardly touched your food.'

Dominic gave a thin smile. 'I wasn't hungry, old man,' he said evenly. 'It's too hot for eating.' He paused before raising his glass to his lips again. 'Particularly when you're wearing a suit.'

'Then get changed!' exclaimed Jacob at once. 'You know I'm expecting you to give Cleo a tour of San Clemente later this afternoon.'

'Oh, that's not necessary—' began Cleo hurriedly, but her grandfather ignored her.

'Me, I'm going to have a rest.' Jacob blew out a breath. 'But you're right. It is hot.'

Cleo turned her head to look at him, aware of an anxiety that was as unexpected as it was misplaced. She hardly knew him, she thought, yet she already felt concerned about him.

Dominic was concerned, too. Putting down his wine glass, he said, 'Perhaps you ought to get Sam to take you back to Magnolia Hill.'

'I can rest here just as well as at Magnolia Hill,' Jacob retorted shortly. 'Just help me down to the cabin, will you, Dom? It'll be cooler below deck.'

Cleo chewed anxiously at her lower lip as Dominic got up and helped his grandfather from his chair. One of the crew appeared, possibly expecting to clear the table, but Jacob only waved the man away.

'Cleo and Dom haven't finished,' he said, albeit a little breathlessly as his grandson supported him towards the stairs to the lower deck. 'Bring my granddaughter some coffee, will you? I think she'd prefer that to the wine.'

By the time Dominic came back, Cleo was sipping her second cup of coffee.

Her eyes darted instantly to his dark face, the enquiry evident in her troubled gaze. 'Is he all right?' she asked, putting her cup down as he crossed the deck towards her. 'The cabins are air-conditioned, aren't they? He'll be able to breathe more easily if the air is cooler.'

'Yeah, he'll be OK.' Dominic flung himself back into his chair and regarded her with an intensity of purpose she couldn't possibly sustain. 'How about you?'

'Me?' Cleo considered picking up her cup again, if only for protection, but she was afraid she might spill its contents. 'I'm OK.' She glanced determinedly about her. 'This certainly is a beautiful place.'

'Yes, it is.' Dominic pulled in a long breath and then went for the jugular. 'I wondered if you'd come.'

Cleo's eyes widened. 'Your grandfather invited me,' she said, and he noted she was back to saying 'your' grandfather and not 'my'. 'Besides, I wanted to see something of the island before I leave.'

Dominic's stomach hollowed. 'You're leaving!'

'In a few days, yes,' said Cleo, concentrating on her finger nudging at her saucer. 'I'd have thought you'd be pleased. If I'm not here, I'm not a threat, am I?'

'A threat!' Dominic's tone hardened. 'A threat to whom?'

Cleo pressed her lips together. 'You know.'

'What the hell's that supposed to mean?' Dominic stared at her, his eyes as cold as green ice. 'If you're implying that I might be upset if the old man decides to leave all his money to you—'

'No!' Cleo had to look at him now, anguish in her dark gaze. 'I'd never think anything like that.' She licked her lips with an agitated tongue. 'You can't think I want Jacob's money! Any of it! I shouldn't be here. I don't belong here. I—I just want to get on with my life.'

'This is your life now,' stated Dominic harshly. He hated the look of horror he'd brought to her face. But she had to understand that Jacob wasn't about to let her go, not without a whole raft of conditions. 'And you do belong here, Cleo. As much as any of us, actually.'

'No—'

'Yes.' With some reluctance Dominic got up from his seat and came to take the one his grandfather had vacated beside her. 'You're Robert's daughter. You can't get away from that. Jacob won't let you.'

Cleo blew out an unsteady breath and Dominic realised she was trembling. Tiny goosebumps had blossomed all over those pale almond shoulders, enveloping the smooth skin of her throat and puckering the rounded curve of her breasts.

And he had to touch her.

To comfort her, he defended himself. But the minute his hand contacted the fine bones of her shoulder, he wanted to do so much more.

In consequence, his voice was harsher than it should have been when he said, 'Is the prospect of staying here so terrible?'

Cleo glanced sideways at him. 'Not terrible, no,' she said tensely. 'But, please, let me go. This isn't helping anyone.'

It's helping me, thought Dominic unevenly, aware of his pulsing arousal.

But she was right. He was behaving like an idiot.

Yet, 'Don't you like me touching you?' he asked thickly, all too aware of the warmth of her bare thigh brushing his trousered leg. 'That's not the impression I got before.'

'Bastard!'

The word was barely audible, but the way she thrust back her chair and got to her feet showed how angry she was. Casting a contemptuous glance over her shoulder, she strode across the deck to the rail, and for a moment Dominic had the uneasy feeling that she intended to jump over the side.

But all she did was grip the rail with both hands and stare out across the water. He guessed her knuckles must be white, judging by the taut muscles tensing in her arms. The stiff line of her spine was eloquent of the resentment she was feeling, the sweet curve of her buttocks above those spectacular thighs made him itch to cup them in his hands.

Dear God!

He dragged his hands through his hair, aware that this wasn't the way he'd intended to play it. Dammit, she had a low enough opinion of him as it was without him making it ten times worse. Yet something about her got under his skin. When he was with her, he couldn't think about anything—or anyone—else.

Common sense was telling him to go and get changed into something cooler and take her into town. He'd promised his grandfather he'd look after her, and that didn't include touching her every chance he got.

Getting to his feet, he stood for a moment regarding that

rigid back, and then, almost of their own volition, his feet moved in her direction.

He stopped directly behind her, but she didn't turn. She must have heard his approach, he thought impatiently, waving the ever-attentive waiter away. The soles of his Oxfords made a distinct sound against the floor of the deck.

'Talk to me,' he said, his breath fluttering the wisps of sable silk that had escaped her scarf. 'Dammit, Cleo, I'm not the only one involved here. You wanted me yesterday morning. You can't deny it. If I hadn't called a halt…'

Cleo clamped her jaws together. She had nothing to say to him. But he was right. However passionately she might try to convince herself that he'd been totally to blame for what had happened, nothing could alter the fact that she'd been completely blown away by his kisses, had been drowning in the sensuous beauty of his mouth.

Her silence angered Dominic. Drawing the wrong conclusions, he did something he would never have done if she'd only admitted there were faults on both sides.

Moving closer, he placed a hand on the rail at either side of her. Now she was imprisoned against the chrome-plated barrier, his lean body taut against her back.

She moved then, tried to turn, but he wouldn't let her. With the scent of her warm body rising to his nostrils and the agitated movements she was making only adding to his unwilling response, there was no way he was going to let her go.

Pressing closer, he let her feel the unmistakable thrust of his arousal. Wedged one leg between hers to feel her sensual heat.

The little moan that issued from her lips when he bent his head and bit the soft skin at the side of her neck was almost his undoing.

It was so fragile, so anguished, and a knot twisted in his belly at the sound. But the desire to turn her round and feel her breasts pucker against his chest was consuming any lingering sense he had left.

'Dominic…'

Her whispered protest only added to the urgent need he had to touch her. The sinuous pressure of her thighs against his pelvis almost drove him crazy with need.

'I want you,' he said, his voice barely recognisable to his own ears, it was so thick and hoarse with emotion. 'I don't care about anything else. I just want to feel you naked in my arms.'

'And then what?' Cleo challenged him unsteadily, even as her treacherous body arched back against him.

She so much wanted to give in. But she had to remember who he was, *what* he was: a man who apparently cared for nothing but his own needs.

She took a deep breath. 'Perhaps you're thinking, like mother, like daughter. That I'm no better than Celeste. That just because a white man looked at her—a married man, moreover—she was happy to let him screw her brains out.'

'No!'

Dominic swore then, his voice harsh with self-loathing. Hauling her round to face him, he grasped her tilted chin in one less-than-gentle hand.

'D'you think that's what all this is about?' he demanded, trying to ignore her quivering lips, her eyes, that were the mirror of her soul. 'Some sick desire to follow in my father's footsteps?' His jaw clenched. 'For God's sake, Cleo, I thought you knew me better than that.'

Cleo trembled. 'But I don't know you at all!' she exclaimed, her hands gripping his biceps, feeling the muscles grow taut beneath the fine cotton of his shirt. 'I don't know anything about you.'

She was trying to hold him back, but it was a losing battle. He was so much stronger than she was, so much more determined to have his way.

'You do know me,' he said savagely. His thumb scraped painfully across her lower lip. 'Dammit, you know how I feel about you.'

'Do I?'

Her eyes widened and now he could see tears sparkling in

the corners. And the desire he'd had to hurt her as she was hurting him was strangled by his need to comfort her.

'Cleo—'

'You want I should clear now, Mr Dominic, sir?'

Dominic couldn't believe it. One of the yacht's younger—less experienced—stewards had appeared at the top of the steps that led down to the domestic area of the vessel carrying a tray.

Forced to let go of Cleo, Dominic swung round, ready to deliver a cutting denial. But Cleo's hand on his sleeve was a silent rebuke.

'All right,' he muttered. 'Why not?' He gave the youth an affirming nod. 'I guess we're finished here.'

Then, striding away towards the companionway, he cast a look back at Cleo. 'Wait for me,' he commanded harshly. 'I won't be long.'

CHAPTER ELEVEN

THE phone rang as Dominic was getting ready to go for his morning run.

He was tempted to ignore it. But it just might be his grandfather, and he and the old man were not on such good terms at the moment.

Calling to Ambrose, his houseman, that he'd get it, Dominic returned to the foyer and picked up the receiver.

'Yeah,' he said flatly, and then stifled an oath when Sarah came on the line.

He'd managed to avoid talking to Sarah for the last couple of days. He'd had Hannah tell her he was out when she'd rung him at the office, and Ambrose had orders not to tell anyone but Jacob that he was in the house.

He'd known Cleo wouldn't ring. Since that afternoon on the yacht, he'd neither seen nor spoken to her. Mostly because Jacob had ordered him to stay away from Magnolia Hill.

She'd been gone when he'd returned to the sundeck that day. The young steward had stammered out the news that the young lady had walked off into town.

Dominic had known right away that he hadn't a hope in hell of finding her in the busy little town. The straw market adjoined the harbour and it was the easiest thing in the world to get lost among the many booths and stalls.

Besides, he'd suspected she'd find some way to get back to Magnolia Hill, and she had. She evidently hadn't wanted to disturb her grandfather, but equally she'd have rather done anything than wait for him.

Which, of course, was why he and Jacob were barely speaking to one another. Jacob had had no hesitation in blaming Dominic for Cleo's sudden departure from the yacht.

'You'd better keep your hands off her in future,' he'd warned his grandson, not at all convinced by Dominic's explanation that Cleo had left the yacht of her own volition. 'If anything happens to that girl, boy, I'll know exactly who to blame.'

Dominic had had to accept that that was fair comment. And he had to admit that neither of them had known a minute's peace until Serena had rung to say Cleo had returned to the house in a taxi.

She'd been curious, too, and he'd thought he could imagine the subsequent conversation between her and his mother. But he'd been so relieved that Cleo was home safely, nothing else had mattered.

'Dominic; darling.' Sarah's voice was amazingly amicable in the circumstances. He'd have expected accusations and tantrums, but instead she sounded much the same as she always did. 'What have you been doing? I've been trying to reach you for days.'

Dominic blew out a weary breath. 'I'm sorry about that,' he said evenly. 'Was there something urgent you wanted to speak to me about?'

'Nothing really, darling.' Sarah was a little less conciliatory now. 'Where have you been? I even asked your grandfather where you were, but he said he hadn't seen you either.'

Did he, now?

Dominic's jaw compressed. He wouldn't have put it past the old man to make some provocative comment and enjoy the fallout.

But it seemed Jacob was prepared to let his grandson lead his own life, so long as it didn't involve Cleo. And so long as he wasn't expected to pick up the pieces if anything went wrong.

'I've been pretty busy,' he said at last, despising himself for prevaricating. He was going to have to be honest with her, so why not now?

But how the hell did you tell someone that you were in lust with another woman? That since meeting Cleo, he hadn't been able to think of anyone else?

Besides, as he kept telling himself, this crazy infatuation would pass. It had to. Once Cleo returned to England, he'd get over this madness that was controlling his life.

If she returned to England.

He scowled. If his grandfather had his way, she'd only return there long enough to settle her affairs before returning to San Clemente and making her home here.

'So what does that mean?' Sarah's voice was considerably cooler now. 'I was under the impression that you had executive assistants and managers to handle the day-to-day operation of the company for you.' She paused. 'Or is what you're really saying that you're so busy with your grandfather's houseguest that you haven't got time for me?'

Dominic stifled a groan, raking a frustrated hand through the thickness of his hair. How was he supposed to answer that?

The truth was, she was right, but he couldn't tell her that on the telephone. That was the cowardly way out, and, although he might be a bastard, he had no intention of deliberately hurting her.

'OK,' he said at last. 'I suppose I have been neglecting you lately. But…' He closed his eyes for a moment, trying to decide how best to proceed. 'I knew you didn't like Cleo—'

'I didn't say that.'

Sarah didn't let him finish, and Dominic heaved a sigh. 'You didn't have to,' he said. 'That night at Magnolia Hill, you practically ignored her.'

'All right.' Sarah seemed to realise she couldn't go on denying it. 'I don't like her. I admit it. You mother doesn't like her either. All that fuss over one dinner party!'

'A dinner party that was supposed to have been arranged to

welcome Cleo to the island,' retorted Dominic, feeling his control slipping again. 'Not as a reason for you and my mother to sharpen your claws.'

'Dominic!'

Sarah caught her breath now, and Dominic realised he'd gone too far.

'Yeah, yeah,' he said wearily. 'That was a little harsh.'

'A little?'

'All right, a lot.' He blew out a breath. 'I'm sorry. I guess I'm not in the best of moods at the moment.'

Sarah hesitated. 'Is it her; Cleo?' she ventured after a moment. 'I mean, I suppose it is pretty difficult for you, her staying at Magnolia Hill and all. You and your grandfather have always been so close, and if he's thinking of making her his heir—'

'Where the hell did that come from?' Dominic demanded angrily.

But he knew. His mother. They were her words, not Sarah's.

'I just meant—'

'Yeah, I know what you meant.'

Dominic's tone was harsh, but somehow he managed to get a handle on his emotions. It wasn't her fault and he had to stop behaving as if it was.

'Look,' he said, immediately regretting it, 'are you free this evening?'

Sarah gasped. 'I—I think so.'

'Good.' Dominic tamped down his disappointment. 'Then how about we have dinner together? I've heard there's a new restaurant opened on Bay Street—'

'I'd prefer it if we could have dinner at Turtle Cove,' Sarah interrupted him appealingly. 'It seems ages since we've had dinner together. Just the two of us, you know. Alone.'

Dominic bit back an instinctive denial. 'Why not?' he conceded after a moment, realising it would be easier to talk without an audience. 'Shall we say—eight o'clock? Eight-thirty?'

'So late?' Sarah was plaintive. But then, with a little sigh of resignation, she agreed. 'Eight o'clock. I'll look forward to it.'

'Yeah.' Dominic almost put down the receiver without responding. 'Um—so will I.'

Cleo left the house by the back entrance.

She'd discovered there was a second staircase that descended to a rear lobby, and she'd become accustomed to using it whenever she didn't want to encounter anyone else.

Which usually only happened after her grandfather had retired for the night.

During the day she'd adapted to life at Magnolia Hill very well, she thought. Perhaps the fact that there was a limit to the length of time she would stay here was a contributing factor.

As things stood, she'd made it plain to Jacob that she didn't feel she belonged here. This was Serena's home, not hers. And so far he seemed to have accepted that.

Consequently, her relations with the other women in the household had improved considerably. Since their confrontation over the lunch table, even Lily seemed to have revised her opinion of her. So much so that on a couple of occasions recently she'd actually thawed enough to ask Cleo about her life in England.

If Cleo suspected that Lily's intention was to remind her of her roots, she didn't say anything. And at least both women had stopped regarding her as a threat to their own positions in Jacob's life. She didn't think they thought she was a gold-digger any longer. And Jacob was so delighted to have her here that no one wanted to deny him his last chance of happiness.

The only cloud on the horizon was Dominic.

It was several days since she'd seen him; several days since he'd visited Magnolia Hill. She didn't like to think that she was to blame for his apparent estrangement from his grandfather. But deep inside, she knew she was.

There was no one about and Cleo tramped through the dunes

and down onto the beach. Kicking off her flip-flops, she allowed her toes to curl into the moist sand.

Heaven, she thought. She would miss this when she went back to England. Would miss a lot, if she was honest. She'd begun to care about her grandfather, and it troubled her that when she returned to England she might never see him again.

She sniffed, aware that she was suddenly near to tears. She hadn't thought she was a particularly emotional person, but since she'd come to San Clemente she found her eyes filling with tears at the most inappropriate moments.

Like just after Dominic had kissed her for the first time, she mused, when she'd stumbled, wet and dishevelled, back to the house.

And after their confrontation on the yacht. When she'd been desperate to escape the probable outcome of his lovemaking.

No, not his lovemaking, she corrected herself fiercely as she started to walk along the shoreline. They hadn't made love, thank God, although goodness knew she'd wanted to.

She'd wanted him, she admitted now. Just as he'd said. But she'd denied it. Though not in words, she thought bitterly. Just by running away. And how convincing was that?

She'd been walking briskly for some time when all at once she realised she was running out of beach. A rocky groyne provided a natural barrier between this cove and the next. And, because she felt too edgy to go back yet, she slipped on her flip-flops again and climbed up onto the rocks.

It was higher than she'd thought, and she was glad she'd taken the time to change before heading out. Cotton shorts and a strappy vest were far more suitable for rock-climbing than the camisole dress she'd worn for dinner with her grandfather.

The deserted strip of beach beyond the barrier was appealing. Moonlight illuminated a stretch of sand similar to the one she'd just walked along, and the idea of going further was tempting.

No one would miss her, if she was late back, she knew. Lily had gone out for the evening and Serena had already retired to her rooms for the night. She, too, was supposed to be having an early night, but there was no reason to feel guilty, just because she'd left the house.

Clambering down the other side of the outcrop, she bit her lip when she almost lost her footing. She grimaced. It would be just like her to fall and sprain her ankle; to have to spend the night camped out on the rocks.

But nothing more daunting happened. She gained the beach at the other side of the rocks and once again kicked off her sandals. She dismissed the sudden thought that she might be trespassing on someone's private property. If she was discovered, she had a perfectly good excuse.

She'd walked perhaps a couple of hundred yards when she saw the house just ahead of her.

She'd been thinking of other things, not least how she was going to feel when she got back to England, and the sudden appearance of the building caused her to come to an abrupt stop.

It was standing on a slight rise. Single-storeyed; built of mellow brick. Perhaps not as big as Magnolia Hill, but still immensely impressive.

She caught her breath in alarm. So she was trespassing, she thought. Clearly, this beach belonged to the house.

And it was occupied, too. Lights streamed from a dozen windows, highlighting the terrace gardens, giving colour to the moon-bleached vegetation that hedged a cantilevered deck.

Sliding glass doors to the deck stood open. And even as she watched, her eyes wide and incredulous, a man and a woman emerged from the house to confront one another across its lamp-lit area.

A man Cleo knew only too well, she realised disbelievingly. And a woman she hardly knew at all.

Sarah.

Cleo knew she should retreat. If she slunk away into the shadows, no one need ever know she'd been there. This was evidently Dominic's house, Dominic's beach, Dominic's property.

The house he must have left that morning when she'd encountered him on the beach below Magnolia Hill.

But she didn't move.

Dominic and Sarah were arguing.

Or rather Sarah was arguing. Dominic's stillness was an indication of his mood. Sarah kept waving her arms about, shifting from one foot to the other. Making accusations, if her pointing finger was any guide. Though Cleo knew her judgement could be sadly flawed.

Then Sarah stepped forward and slapped Dominic's face.

The sound was clearly audible and Cleo pressed her hand to her mouth to silence her automatic gasp of dismay. For heaven's sake, what was going on?

She half expected Dominic to respond then. In her world, women didn't get away with striking their partners without expecting some kind of retaliation.

But Dominic didn't move. Didn't do anything. And Sarah burst into uncontrollable sobbing, making Cleo feel even worse for witnessing her distress.

She had to leave, she told herself. Now. This minute. She was no better than a voyeur, watching something she had no right to see.

But couples had arguments all the time, she assured herself as a form of justification. Though that didn't excuse her behaviour. Not at all. So why didn't she just go back to Magnolia Hill?

'Don't you have anything else to say?'

Sarah's words were suddenly audible and once again Cleo stifled a gasp. Instead of backing away, she'd moved forward, and now only the bushes that grew in the angle of the deck protected her from discovery.

To her horror, Dominic's gaze turned towards the garden then, and she felt a momentary sense of panic that somehow he'd seen her and was about to expose her.

But then Sarah spoke again, and his attention was distracted.

'I'm leaving,' she declared, scrubbing at her eyes with a

damp tissue. 'I don't think there's any point in my staying any longer, do you?'

'Probably not.'

Dominic's response was spoken in a neutral tone and Sarah let out an anguished cry.

'You're a bastard, Dominic Montoya,' she accused him bitterly. 'And I hate you!'

Once again, Dominic made no response and Sarah's face contorted.

'I can't talk to you when you're in this mood,' she said angrily. 'I'm going home.'

Pushing past him, she strode into the house. A few moments later, Cleo heard the sound of a car's engine, and then the unmistakable squeal of rubber as the vehicle took off.

Only then did she realise she'd been holding her breath. Expelling it weakly, she allowed her head to tip forward, feeling a distinct surge of relief.

She hadn't realised how tightly she'd been wound until the tension eased, and she moistened lips that had become dry and parched.

'You can come up now.'

Her relief was short-lived.

Her head jerked up to find Dominic looking down at her. Arms resting on the rail of the deck, he was regarding her with a mixture of curiosity and derision. And she realised that when she'd thought he'd seen her, he had.

CHAPTER TWELVE

CLEO tried to gather her scattered wits.

'Perhaps I don't want to come up,' she said, tugging the ponytail she'd made of her hair with nervous fingers. Then, because curiosity was a two-way street, 'How did you know I was here?'

'Oh, please.' Dominic's lazy voice scraped across her nerves, making her heart beat even faster than it was doing already. 'If you want to go sneaking about, don't wear a white top.'

Cleo glanced down at her vest. 'It's not white,' she said pedantically. 'It's cream.'

'Oh, well, excuse me.' Dominic was sarcastic now. 'Don't wear a *cream* top, then.'

Cleo squared her shoulders. 'In any case, I wasn't sneaking about,' she added defensively. 'I didn't know this was your house.'

'No?'

'Not until I saw you, no.' She was indignant. 'You usually come to Magnolia Hill by car.'

'Yeah.' Dominic conceded her point. 'Half a dozen miles by road. Less than a mile across the sand. Go figure.'

Cleo drew in a breath and took a step backward. 'I think I ought to be going—'

'So you don't want to see where I live?'

Of course she did. Cleo swallowed. But, 'Not particularly,' she said tightly. 'Serena will be wondering where I am.'

'You think?' Dominic's dark brows arched at the blatant lie. 'If I know my dear aunt, she's probably tucked up in bed at this moment, watching her soaps. Serena's a great soap fan. Did you know?'

Cleo shrugged, causing one of the bootlace straps to tip off her shoulder. Hurriedly replacing it, she said, 'She went to her room. That's all I know.'

'Well, take my word for it.' Dominic scowled, impatient with himself for getting involved with her again. 'So—do you want to have a drink with me? A non-alcoholic drink,' he amended swiftly. 'Then I'll drive you home.'

'I can take myself home, thank you,' said Cleo firmly, but her eyes drifted irresistibly towards the flight of wooden steps that led up to the deck.

She'd be a fool if she accepted any invitation from him, she told herself fiercely. She didn't trust him, and after the way he'd just treated Sarah...

'Better you than me, then,' Dominic remarked carelessly, and she had to concentrate hard to remember what she'd said. 'The tide's coming in,' he continued. 'The rocks are dangerously slippery when they're wet.'

Now, why had he said that? Dominic wondered half frustratedly. Why the hell was he persisting with this when it was obvious she was just as dangerous to his peace of mind?

Cleo had turned round now and was looking rather anxiously towards the ocean. Sure enough, the distance, between where she was standing and the water, had definitely narrowed in the last few minutes.

He felt her indecision. Felt it in the looks she cast up at him, the uneven breath she blew out before she spoke again.

'Why—why should I trust you to take me home?' she asked, but he could tell that she was weakening. 'You were cruel to Sarah. She was in tears when she left here.'

Dominic grunted. The nerve of the woman.

'I have no intention of discussing my relationship with Sarah with you,' he stated flatly. He turned away from the rail. 'Do what you like.'

Cleo sighed and looked along the beach. She could see that the waves were indeed starting to splash over the rocky promontory. And realised that to return to Magnolia Hill that way would be far more scary than she'd thought.

Dominic had entered his living room and was pouring himself another whisky when he heard her coming up the steps outside.

Swallowing a mouthful of the single malt, he stared grimly at his reflection in the mirror above the fieldstone hearth. And scowled at his image, wondering why the hell he hadn't just pretended not to see her.

Inviting her into his house had to be the craziest thing he'd ever done. He didn't want her here, he told himself. He didn't want to be reminded of her every time a shadow moved across his vision, didn't want to smell her distinctive fragrance in places he'd hitherto regarded as his own personal territory.

He didn't want her making a mockery of his life.

Despite the sexual chemistry between them—and he couldn't deny that—there was no way they could have an affair. She'd never forgive his father for the way he'd treated her mother and, if history was repeating itself, she wanted no part of it.

But he still wanted her. That was a given. Wanted her with an urgency that he'd never felt before.

He wondered how she'd feel if he told her that the reason Sarah had rushed out of here in tears was because, despite all her efforts, she'd failed to arouse even a trace of the excitement he was feeling now.

It had not been a pleasant evening. Dominic hated having to play the villain. Usually, his relationships ended by mutual consent.

Or did they? Perhaps he'd only been kidding himself. If Sarah was to be believed, his reputation was in shreds. But then, that begged the question of why she had gone out with him. And why she should be so bitter because they were breaking up.

Certainly, Dominic had begun to wish he'd insisted on meeting her at a restaurant. Surely with other diners around, Sarah wouldn't have resorted to threats. She'd actually accused him of cheating on her. She'd had some wild notion that he'd already slept in Cleo's bed.

Wild indeed!

Still, threatening to tell his grandfather about the affair he was purportedly having with Cleo had been one step too far. And, although she'd evidently regretted it afterwards, Dominic had had enough.

She should have resorted to tears sooner, he thought with a trace of self-mockery. Few men were immune to a woman's tears.

He heard footsteps crossing the deck and then silence. Cleo had paused between the sliding doors and was waiting for him to acknowledge her.

He didn't turn. Not immediately. Let her stew for a while, he thought savagely. He'd had a basinful of that, goodness knew.

But then she cleared her throat, a nervous little sound, and his stomach muscles clenched. He couldn't do this, he thought firmly. What the hell did she think was going on here?

A pulse in his jaw jerked as he swung round to face her. 'Come in, why don't you?' he said harshly. 'And shut the door before we get eaten alive.'

Cleo hesitated a moment. Then she stepped inside onto cool Italian marble tiles, and slid the window closed behind her.

She was in a huge room, a beautiful room, with a high, arching ceiling. Dark wood predominated, starkly elegant against pale upholstered walls.

There were several chairs and sofas positioned about the room, some in honey-soft leather, others in plush velvet or brocade. And a thick Chinese rug in shades of cream and topaz. The large stone fireplace was presently filled with exotic blossoms: anthurium and bird of paradise; delicate orchids and calla lilies. And her own reflection was thrown back at her in the mirror above the mantel.

Dominic was standing beside the fireplace, a half-filled tumbler of what she guessed was whisky in his hand. He wasn't wearing a tie and his shirt was half-open down his chest. The shirt was black, like his trousers, and exposed a triangle of brown flesh lightly covered with coarse dark hair.

Lord, but he looked good, Cleo thought, feeling her awareness of him deepen. There was a heaviness in her limbs, a disturbing sense of moisture between her legs. She wanted to sit down, rather badly. If for no other reason than to hide the treacherous tremor in her knees.

She must keep her head, she warned herself fiercely. But she was beginning to understand how Celeste must have felt when Robert Montoya had taken her to his bed. Celeste must have tried to resist, to keep her head in the face of enormous provocation. But ultimately she'd surrendered to something maybe stronger than herself.

Meanwhile Dominic was facing his own demons. He knew, better than anyone, how dangerous the present situation was. This had never happened to him before, but that didn't alter the fact that there was a certain inevitability to it.

He could feel his own need in the thickness of his erection, and marvelled that only minutes before, when Sarah had been trying to arouse him, he had felt no reaction at all.

Hot blood pounded through his veins, insistent, demanding, intense. He felt both angry and vulnerable. Was he no longer in control of his own life?

Cleo was waiting for him to say something, and he nodded somewhat offhandedly towards a chilled cabinet standing at the opposite side of the room.

'Can I get you a drink? A *soft* drink,' he corrected himself with a tight smile.

'Thank you.' Cleo was struggling to remember why she'd come here. It certainly hadn't been her most sensible action to date. 'Um—a cola would be good.' She paused. 'If you have one.'

A cola!

Dominic shook his head as he crossed the room to open the cabinet. Pulling out a can, he reflected that at least there was no danger of her getting drunk and doing something rash.

Like coming on to him…

All the same, having her in his house was a torment. She looked so incredibly sexy in the skimpy vest and shorts. Unfortunately, he could remember only too well how she'd looked without any clothes. That creamy almond skin; the raw temptation of her mouth.

Frustration gripped him, and pulling the tab on the can, he poured it into a glass. Adding a straw, he decided she could have this one drink, then he'd take her back to Magnolia Hill. They'd both be infinitely safer with other people around.

His fingers brushed hers as he handed her the glass and immediately his good intentions foundered. He felt the contact radiating heat right to his groin.

He knew he should move away, should put the width of the room between them, but he just stood there. Watching as she sucked the ice-cold cola through the straw, imagining where he'd like to feel those sucking lips.

His next words shocked him almost as much as they shocked her.

'Let's go to bed,' he said abruptly, knowing there was no point in denying what he really wanted.

Cleo's eyes widened in disbelief. Almost choking, she whispered, 'Wh-what did you say?'

As if there was any doubt about it.

'I think you heard what I said,' retorted Dominic huskily, setting down his own glass and taking hers out of her unresisting fingers. 'I said, let's go to bed. I want to make love with you.'

Cleo looked uncomprehending. This couldn't be happening, she told herself. Not after everything that had gone before. He knew how she felt about Robert Montoya's relationship with Celeste, with her *mother*. How could he ask her to go to bed with him knowing how that other affair had turned out?

It didn't matter that his words had sent the blood streaming through her veins like wildfire. Or that, only moments before, she'd been having similar thoughts about him.

She was ashamed of herself for even thinking such things, particularly after the way he'd treated his girlfriend. She should be feeling sorry for Sarah; despising Dominic for attempting to use her to assuage his obvious frustration.

Her breathing had quickened and now she said a little breathlessly, 'What's the matter? Did Sarah turn you down?'

Dominic's green eyes grew icy. 'You can't turn down something that doesn't exist,' he said harshly. 'If you want chapter and verse, it was Sarah who was frustrated, not me.'

'But—why?' Cleo was confused. 'I—I thought you wanted her.'

'I thought so, too,' said Dominic flatly. 'But unfortunately I don't.' His eyes softened. 'I want you.'

Cleo drew a trembling breath. 'You—you don't mean that.'

'Oh, come on.' Dominic was impatient now. 'You can't deny there's something going on between us. You felt it that morning on the beach and you knew it when we were on the yacht. That's why you ran away.'

Cleo swallowed. 'I didn't run away.'

'Well, your grandfather sure as hell didn't take you.'

'Jacob was sleeping. I didn't want to disturb him.'

'Yeah, right.' Dominic's response was sardonic. 'And I suppose you didn't hear me ask you to wait for me.'

'I heard.'

'So?'

Cleo was defensive. 'I—got bored.'

'With me?'

Cleo couldn't answer that. Shaking her head, she turned away.

Never with you, she thought achingly, aware that, slowly but surely, he was wearing her resistance down.

'I'll take that as a no, then, shall I?' he asked softly, and the draught of his breath across her skin made her realise he had come to stand close behind her.

'You—you can take it any way you like,' she mumbled, feeling his heat surrounding her, enveloping her. Then, with a distinct effort, 'This—this isn't going to happen, Dominic.'

'Isn't it?'

Her shoulder was just too tempting and, bending his head, Dominic allowed his tongue to stroke her bare skin.

'N—no,' she said unconvincingly. 'Please—don't do that.'

'Why?' Dominic slipped the strap of the vest off her shoulder, his body quickening when he discovered she wasn't wearing a bra. 'Don't you like me touching you?'

Too much, thought Cleo tremulously, resisting the urge to give in to the torment and rest back against him.

'Come on,' he persisted, his hand slipping from her shoulder to the swollen curve of her breast. 'You want me. Why don't you admit it? And you know I want you.'

'I—I can't—'

'Yes, you can.' Dominic's arm slipped possessively about her waist, drawing her back against him. 'Feel that?' he said thickly. 'Then tell me you don't feel the same.'

'I don't.'

'Well, not precisely the same, obviously,' he muttered impatiently. 'But I bet if I slipped my finger beneath the hem of your shorts—'

'Don't you dare!'

For a moment indignation brought her to her senses, but when she would have twisted away from him, he wouldn't let her.

'Cool it,' he said, and, to her dismay, he peeled the other strap off her shoulder.

She tried to clutch the folds of the vest against her, but his hands were insistent. Cupping her breasts, he said hoarsely, 'Don't play with me, Cleo. I need you.'

'You don't need me,' protested Cleo fiercely. 'You want to have sex with me. Let's tell it as it is, as that seems to be the way you like it.'

'OK.' Dominic stifled a groan as her rigid body pressed into him. 'OK, I want to have sex with you.' He made a bitter sound. 'Please don't tell me you've never had sex with a man before.'

Cleo trembled. 'I'm not denying it,' she said. Although the couple of occasions she had allowed a man into her bed had hardly been memorable.

'So?'

'So what?'

'So why don't we just do it and put us both out of our misery?' he demanded unsteadily. 'It's what I want. It's what you want—'

'It's not what I wan—' she began, but she didn't finish her sentence.

With a groan of desperation, Dominic twisted her round in his arms and stifled her protest with his mouth.

Cleo's resistance crumbled. With Dominic's mouth hard on hers she could hardly breathe, let alone think. His tongue plunged hot and hungry between her teeth and she sank weakly against him.

It was all Dominic could do to remain upright. The temptation to throw her down on the Chinese carpet beneath their feet was very appealing, to peel those tantalising shorts down her legs and—

But that was as far as he dared take it without losing what little control he had left. Instead, with his mouth still plundering hers, he swept her up into his arms and carried her out of the living room. The corridor to his bedroom had never seemed so long, but at last he was able to push open the door.

Ambrose had switched on the lamps in the room, but the sheers at the windows had been drawn back and darkness pressed at the panes. A huge bed, covered with a thick chocolate coverlet, occupied a prominent position, and, kicking the door closed behind him, Dominic carried Cleo to the bed and lowered her onto it.

The bedcover was cool against Cleo's back, and when Dominic straightened she was able to take in the beauty of the room.

Pale wood, wide windows, a velvet-soft carpet on the floor. This was his bedroom, she thought, smoothing her damp palms against the figured silk of the coverlet. This was his bed, this huge expanse of thick, springy mattress and soft, downy pillows, wooden rails at both the head and the foot.

This was where he slept.

Where he'd probably slept with Sarah.

So why didn't it appal her that she was here?

It should.

But Sarah need never know, she told herself.

And wasn't that exactly what her father must have told her mother?

CHAPTER THIRTEEN

DOMINIC peeled off his shirt and came down beside her, and her eyes were briefly dazzled by the beauty of the man. He was all brown, tanned flesh, strong and dark and masculine. And he wanted her, Cleo Novak, she thought incredulously.

How amazing was that?

He moved over her, straddling her thighs. His trousered crotch was rough against her soft skin, but she barely noticed. Then he bent and rubbed his hair-roughened chest against her, warm, taut muscle against her naked breasts.

'God you have no idea how much I've wanted to do this,' he said hoarsely, and Cleo closed her eyes.

She suspected she had a fair idea, she thought. Probably as much as she had wanted him to touch her. Her head was spinning with the nearness of him, with the spicy scent of shaving soap and man.

When he drew back to caress her breasts with his hands, she trembled. His thumbs abraded the swollen peaks and she felt the flood of her own arousal.

'This—this is crazy, you know that,' she breathed, opening her eyes when she felt his mouth take the place of his fingers. Then, catching her breath, 'In heaven's name, what are you doing?'

Dominic lifted his head to give her a smouldering look. 'Don't you like it?' he asked, blowing softly on the damp tip of the breast he'd been suckling, and she gave a weak nod of submission.

'No one—no man, that is, or woman either,' she appended hastily, 'has—has ever done that to me before.'

Dominic's expression showed his satisfaction now. 'So you are a virgin, in some ways,' he murmured softly, and she caught her breath.

In lots of ways, she thought, wishing she had more experience in these matters. Wishing, too, that Dominic would take the rest of his clothes off. She felt too vulnerable, too exposed.

But Dominic seemed intent on robbing her of any dignity. Unbuttoning the waistband of her shorts, he pushed them down over her hips. Pushed her bikini briefs with them, she realised, feeling the cool draught of air against her skin.

'Please…' she protested, but Dominic only bent his head and nuzzled the flat plane of her stomach.

'Let me,' he said, his voice thickening, and she felt his fingers part the dusky curls at the apex of her legs and press intimately inside.

He felt her wetness, felt the little jerk she gave when he caressed her. And withdrew his fingers and brought them to his lips.

'Oh, Dominic,' she choked and this time he seemed to understand her feelings.

'Don't stop me, sweetheart,' he whispered. 'You taste as delicious as you look.'

But then, as her eyes widened and hot colour stained her cheeks, he took pity on her. 'OK, OK,' he said, rolling onto his side beside her. Giving her a rueful grin, he quickly unbuckled his belt.

He pushed his trousers down his legs with no trace of embarrassment. He exposed long, powerful limbs, liberally spread with night-dark hair. And Cleo, watching him, was mesmerised by his maleness, by the thick shaft rising proudly from its nest of curling hair.

He was so big, she thought, her heartbeat accelerating. So

big and hard and most definitely aroused. His erection reared its head and she swallowed uneasily. Was she really going to be woman enough for him?

A tiny drop of moisture sparkled on the tip of his erection, and Dominic saw her looking at it, looking at him.

'Did I say I wanted you?' he asked, bending to trace her lips with his tongue.

Then, capturing one of her hands, he closed it around his throbbing shaft. He kissed her again, feeling the innocent slide of her fingers, knowing just how close he was to the edge.

He sucked in a breath. 'Well, let's take that up a stretch,' he said a little raggedly. Her hand was making its own exploration and he knew he couldn't take much more.

He pulled her hair free of its confining band and pushed his hands into its vibrant texture. 'I'm mad for you.' He covered her cheeks and forehead with damp, urgent kisses. 'I want to be inside you, a part of you. I don't want to know where my body ends and yours begins.'

His mouth returned to hers, hot and demanding. And hers opened to him, her tongue seeking his in an eager mating dance. Then he drew back to trail kisses over her breasts and down her quivering body, the rough stubble of his jaw a sexual abrasive against her sensitive skin.

He felt her response in the way her body arched towards him. She didn't hold back, but lifted one leg to wind it seductively about his thigh.

She moaned, an abandoned, sensual little sound that rocked his universe. He knew he'd never wanted any other woman as he wanted her.

When his tongue found her core, she shifted in protest. But without drawing back Dominic parted her womanly folds to reveal her bud, already swollen with need.

'You—you can't,' she gasped, when he nudged her legs apart and she realised his intentions.

'Oh, I can,' he said hoarsely, tasting her essence. 'You're so ready for me.' He felt her buck against him. 'It would be so easy to make you come right now.'

Cleo knew it. Could feel her scattered senses urging him on.

But, 'Not—not like this,' she whispered, clutching handfuls of his hair, trying to drag him up to her. 'Dominic, I want you. I want to feel you inside me. Not—not just your tongue.'

Dominic groaned. 'I know,' he said unsteadily, and with a reluctant sigh he moved over her again. 'But you taste so good, I want more of it. More of everything. More of you.'

Her legs were parted and he slid his hands beneath her bottom to bring her closer. For a moment, she felt a sense of panic, remembering how big he was, wondering if she could do this.

But then, with an ease of movement she could only envy, he allowed his shaft to probe her moist entry. And then thrust smoothly into her slick sheath.

Her body expanded automatically. His thick erection stretched her and filled her with a completeness she'd never felt before.

She caught her breath and immediately he drew back to look down at her. 'Did I hurt you?' he demanded, but the sensual look in her eyes was answer enough.

'No, you didn't hurt me,' she said huskily, framing his anxious face in her palms, brushing an erotic thumb across his lips. 'It's incredible. You're incredible.' Her tongue circled her lips. 'Don't—stop—now.'

'As if I could,' said Dominic a little unsteadily, feeling his body tight against her womb.

He drew back again and then rocked forward, pinning her to the mattress, the friction of their two bodies moving together a tantalising provocation.

But he couldn't prolong the experience. Much as he would have liked to make this first consummation last forever it couldn't be done. Cleo was too hot, too eager, too wickedly delicious to allow him to take his time.

She delighted him, she enchanted him, she taught him there

was as much satisfaction in giving as to receive. His body felt as if it was on fire. The feeling was so intense, he felt there was a danger that they might both go up in flames.

His movements quickened as the urgency of the moment gripped him. Every time he was with this woman, he learned things about himself he'd never known before.

He felt the throbbing pulse of her body, felt the telltale shudder when her climax reached its peak. Felt her muscles clench around him, heard her moan with pleasure, felt the sensual rush of her release.

His own orgasm followed hers almost immediately, the shattering surge of his release arousing an anguished groan from him. His body shook as his seed drained from him, a heated flood that left him weak and trembling with relief.

Cleo's head was spinning dizzily. It had been that way since Dominic started moving, since she'd felt the intimate brush of his pubic hair against her core.

The sensations he'd aroused she hadn't known existed. The climax she'd experienced was like nothing she'd known before.

And she realised that where sex was concerned she was totally out of her depth.

Her body was shaking, still developing the pleasurable pangs of the aftermath of what had happened. Occasionally she felt a twitch deep inside her, felt the softening heat of Dominic's shaft still buried to the hilt.

And remembered with another pang that they'd used no protection. She certainly hadn't thought about it and she suspected it had been the last thing on Dominic's mind when he'd penetrated her, flesh to flesh, skin to skin.

She shivered. It was just as well it wasn't the time of the month when she might have conceived a child, she thought gratefully. It easily could have been, and she could have found herself in exactly the same position as her mother.

The thought was sobering, and with a little wriggle she attempted to get away from him.

But Dominic wasn't asleep. She felt the instant hardening of his erection as he became aware of what she was trying to do.

'Hey,' he said huskily, cupping her face in his hand and rubbing his lips against hers. 'Don't go. I was just enjoying the sensation of lying here, anticipating my next move.' His smile was lazily possessive. 'Now, what do you think it should be?'

'I don't—that is, I have to go,' said Cleo disjointedly. 'Please—move, will you? I want to get up.'

'And I don't want you to get up,' retorted Dominic, his green eyes darkening with obvious impatience. 'I want to make love with you again.' His thumb was rough against her lips. 'All night, if I can make it.'

'No—'

'What do you mean, no?'

Dominic sounded a little peeved now, and Cleo wished she didn't have to do this. But it had gone far further than she had ever intended, and now she had to put an end to it.

'I mean…' She licked her lips, searching for the right words to tell him how she felt. 'This has been really—really—'

'Good? Mediocre? What?' Dominic pushed himself up on his elbows and stared down at her. 'Come on: tell it like it is, why don't you?'

'Oh, please…' Cleo moaned. 'OK, it was—wonderful,' she admitted unwillingly, and then wished she hadn't been so honest when he bent his head and thrust his tongue deep into her mouth.

'Yeah, for me, too,' he muttered, drawing back to caress her face with hungry eyes, and she felt him hardening inside her.

'But…'

He blinked at the negative connotation. 'But what?'

Cleo hesitated. 'It was—good, better than good. But it can't go on.'

'Why not?'

His body was losing that instinctive response and she wished she didn't have to do this.

'You know why,' she told him steadily. 'Not least…' She paused. 'Please—don't make me have to say her name.'

'Sarah?' Dominic scowled. 'Of course, you mean Sarah.'

'Who else?' Cleo gave him a reproving look. 'You can't pretend she doesn't exist.'

'Lord!' Dominic was impatient. 'Do we have to talk about Sarah now?' He blew out a breath. 'You know what, I think you're only using Sarah as an excuse. If you're that desperate to get away from me, be my guest.'

Cleo stared at him for another significant moment. And then, taking him at his word, she gathered all her strength and scrambled out from under him.

Her sudden withdrawal was obviously unexpected, and Dominic rolled onto his back, his hand forming a protective shield for his maleness.

Meanwhile, Cleo hustled across the wide bed in a hasty effort to put some space between them.

Dominic scowled, turning his head to watch her. 'Don't worry,' he said harshly. 'I'm not planning on jumping you, Cleo. For pity's sake, we need to talk about this like adult human beings.'

'Get our stories straight, do you mean?' Cleo wasn't mollified by his appeal. 'Oh, yes, I'm sure that's what your father must have told my mother.'

Dominic's scowl was confused now. 'What's that supposed to mean?'

'She was having an illicit relationship with your father,' retorted Cleo painfully. 'And in many ways, our relationship is the same.'

'No, it's not!'

Dominic hauled himself upright as he spoke, apparently giving up on his attempt to consider her modesty. His eyes were dark with anger as he stared at her and she quivered.

'There's nothing illicit about our relationship. For God's sake, we're two consenting adults. We don't have to consider anyone but ourselves.'

'You think?' Cleo's voice was tremulous. 'I doubt if your mother would agree.'

'My mother has nothing to do with this!' he exclaimed savagely. 'Cleo, I'm a man. I make my own decisions.'

'I had noticed.'

Cleo sniffed again, shaking her head as she looked about her for her clothes. Finding her panties on the floor, she hurriedly put them on without looking at him. She'd never dressed in front of a man before and this was so much worse because of what had been said.

But she could hardly take refuge in his bathroom, even if she wanted to. Not when her clothes were strewn all over his bedroom floor.

'Cleo, please!'

'There's nothing more to say,' she said, rescuing her vest and pulling it over her head.

Her hair was all over the place, but at least she was covered. She spied her shorts lying on the floor at the foot of the bed and snatched them up with some relief.

'Like hell!'

Dominic's anger was obviously growing. He was sitting on the edge of the bed glaring at her, and she couldn't help thinking how sad this whole situation had become.

But why should she expect anything else? She'd broken the rules and now she had to pay for it. It was Sarah she should be feeling sorry for, not herself.

'Cleo,' Dominic began again, 'don't do this to me.' He drew a breath. 'Come on, stay with me tonight.'

'You know I can't.' Hopping from one foot to the other, Cleo struggled to put on her shorts without falling over. 'It was good while it lasted, but don't let's pretend it was anything more than sex. Pure and simple.'

'There was nothing pure about it,' retorted Dominic. 'It wasn't simple either. Not as far as I'm concerned. It was damn complicated. It *is* damn complicated. Do you think I intended this to happen?'

'Do you think I did?' Cleo gasped indignantly. Her fingers stumbled in their attempt to fasten the button at her waist and she muttered a frustrated exclamation. 'Dammit! Dammit! This wasn't my idea.'

'No, it was mine.'

Dominic's tone had gentled, but in her haste to get her shorts on, she barely noticed. However, she had moved nearer to the bed, and now Dominic leant towards her and hooked his fingers into her waistband.

'Don't fasten that,' he said a little thickly, pulling her resisting body between his legs. 'Let me take them off again so you can come back to bed.'

'No!'

Despite the languor that had gripped her as soon as she was close to his naked body again, Cleo managed to overcome it.

Twisting away, she paused when there was some distance between them, and said, 'I want to go back to Magnolia Hill.' She was amazed at the determination in her voice. 'You—you said you'd take me back.'

'Yeah, I did, didn't I?'

Dominic closed his eyes for a long minute. She was right, he thought wearily. He had promised to drive her home. But, dammit, that was before she'd completely blown his mind.

'Cleo, sweetheart—'

He made one final attempt to appeal to her, but she wasn't interested.

'Don't call me that.' She squared her shoulders. 'Are you going to get dressed or do I have to call a cab?'

'Well, good luck with that.' Dominic's tone was dry. 'I don't know any cab drivers on San Clemente who'll turn out after midnight.'

Cleo couldn't believe it. It couldn't be after midnight. But it was.

The little ormolu clock standing on the cabinet beside the bed showed the time as twenty minutes past the hour. She had been away from Magnolia Hill since a little before nine o'clock.

Turning back to Dominic, she placed bravely defiant hands on her hips. 'OK, it's late. So—are you going to take me or do I have to walk?'

Dominic shook his head. 'Like you'd risk walking the better part of six miles in the dark,' he scoffed. 'Even if you knew which way to go—which you don't.'

'I could always try going back the way I came,' she retorted staunchly. 'The tide has probably turned by now.'

'You think?'

Her shoulders abruptly sagged. 'Oh, come on,' she said despairingly. 'Please, Dominic. Don't make me have to beg.'

Dominic's features lost all expression.

With a grim shrug of his shoulders, he got up from the bed. And, although she made a squeaky little sound and leapt back out of his way, he didn't even look at her.

Opening a drawer, he pulled out a pair of cargo shorts and yanked them, commando-style, up his legs. He used his zip but left the button at his waist unfastened. Then, without bothering with a shirt, he nodded pointedly towards the door.

'After you.'

Swallowing the sob that rose in her throat at his sudden coldness, Cleo preceded him from the room. She was half-afraid he might still try to stop her.

Half-afraid he wouldn't.

He didn't.

Barefoot, he led the way across an atrium-roofed foyer to the front doors of the house.

Muted ceiling lights gave the huge reception area a warmly elegant appearance, but Cleo scarcely noticed. She was too wrapped up in her own emotions, her own misery.

This was so much worse than she'd even imagined. Her heart was beating so fast, yet her feet wanted to drag.

She didn't want to leave him, she acknowledged bitterly. She wanted to stay, to be with him. To spend the rest of the night making love with him.

She loved him.

The realisation struck her like a blow to the solar plexus. And it terrified her.

After all her efforts to deny it, to tell herself she'd never do what her mother had done, she'd fallen in love with him.

Oh, she was such a fool!

Dominic didn't love her.

He *wanted* her. She believed that. But wanting wasn't the same as needing someone, and what had just happened had proved it.

CHAPTER FOURTEEN

'IS IT possible for you to arrange for me to go home? Today, preferably.'

It was the next morning and, after making certain enquiries, Cleo had found her way to Serena's apartments.

The older woman had bid her enter her suite, evidently expecting it to be one of the servants. Her eyes had widened considerably when she'd seen Cleo.

'To go home?' she echoed. In a thin silk negligee, Serena had been having breakfast on her balcony. But she'd left the table to answer the door. 'I… Does my father know about this?'

'No one knows,' said Cleo flatly. 'And I wanted to make all the arrangements before I tell Jacob.' She paused. 'I suspect he won't want me to go, but—'

'You suspect!' The emphasis in Serena's voice was much different from her own. 'Cleo, you know he won't agree to this. He wants you to stay here.'

'Well, I can't.' Cleo was determined. 'I'm sorry. I'm going to miss him—miss all of you,' she added a little ruefully. 'But you do understand, don't you? I have my own life. In England.'

Serena's brows drew together. 'I don't know what to say.'

'You don't have to say anything.' Cleo licked her dry lips. 'I think you know, as well as anyone, that my staying here would never have worked.'

'Initially.' Serena hesitated. 'Initially, I'd have said that. Did say it, actually. But things have changed.'

'No, they haven't.'

The last thing Cleo wanted was for Serena to try and persuade her to stay. She'd told herself she was prepared for Jacob's disappointment. Anything else would be too much for her to handle.

And after last night, there was no way she could remain at Magnolia Hill. Not after what had happened. She wasn't her mother. She'd never be satisfied with second-best. And it had been evident from Dominic's attitude that all he wanted was an affair.

She hadn't slept for what was left of the night and, in consequence, she wasn't thinking all that clearly. But one thing seemed perfectly obvious: she had to leave here before she lost all her self-respect.

Last night it had taken quite a hammering. Particularly during that ominously silent drive back to Magnolia Hill. Dominic hadn't spoken, except to advise her to fasten her seat belt, and when he'd dropped her at the house only courtesy had prevented him from driving away before she was safely inside.

As luck would have it, the rear door was still unlocked, and she'd merely lifted a hand in farewell before scuttling through it. She'd heard the SUV's wheels squeal as he'd executed a three-point turn, and prayed no one else had been awake to hear it, too.

And she'd known then how vulnerable she was. She'd wanted to appease him, she admitted painfully. And she *would* give in if she stayed here. It was only a matter of time before he wore her down.

Which mustn't happen.

'Does this have anything to do with Lily?' asked Serena now, and Cleo wondered if she dared use Dominic's mother as an excuse.

But, no. In actual fact, Lily had become the least of her worries. She doubted the other woman would ever like her, but she thought she had gained a bit of respect in her eyes.

Which would soon vanish if she ever found out about her

and Dominic, Cleo conceded bitterly. Lily was prepared to accept that her coming here was not her doing, but her attitude would soon change if she thought Cleo wasn't going back.

'I just want to go home,' Cleo said simply, and Serena shook her head.

'You know my father considers that this is your home, don't you?' she protested. She paused. 'Nobody knows how much time he has left. Couldn't you put your own life on hold for a few more weeks?'

Cleo sighed. 'You know I only got leave of absence for two weeks.'

'But I'm sure, in the circumstances—'

'No.' Cleo hated having to refuse her, to refuse Jacob, but what could she do?

'I have to go back,' she insisted. 'You know people don't accept me here.'

'They're beginning to.' Serena was persuasive. 'You have to give people time to get to know you, Cleo. No one knew of your existence until a few weeks ago.'

'Do you think I've forgotten?'

There was a trace of pain in Cleo's voice now. She'd been sure it wouldn't matter to her, but it did.

And Serena did something Cleo never would have expected. She stepped towards her and enfolded her in her arms.

'You have to put the past behind you, my dear,' she said gently. 'Believe me, we all feel regret for things that we did, things we didn't do. I more than most.'

Cleo had submitted to the embrace, but now she drew back to look at this woman who was, amazingly, her aunt.

'What do you mean?'

'Oh…' Serena pulled a wry face. 'Hasn't my father told you about Michael Cordy?'

A trace of colour entered Cleo's cheeks at her words and Serena nodded her head resignedly.

'I see he has,' she said. 'Did he tell you Michael asked me to marry him? Not once, but several times?' She grimaced.

'And, like a fool, I turned him down. I had the mistaken idea that my father needed me here.'

'I'm sure he did, Serena.' Cleo had never imagined she'd be comforting her aunt. 'When your mother died, he must have been desolate.'

'I suppose he was.' Serena tipped her head from side to side in a gesture that spoke of her uncertainty. 'But I was never woman enough for him. He could always walk all over me. He still does, if I let him.'

'Oh, Serena!' Cleo felt such sympathy for her. 'He loves you. You know he does. Perhaps his illness…'

'Do you honestly think his being ill has made a scrap of difference to the way he thinks of me; the way he thinks of all of us?' Serena was scornful. 'You know, perhaps I shouldn't be trying to persuade you to stay here. Heaven knows, if you did, your life would never be your own.'

Cleo sighed, releasing herself with some reluctance from Serena's arms. Then she put a little space between them.

'I have to go,' she said, hoping the other woman wouldn't ask for any more reasons. 'Will you—do what you can to arrange it?'

'And risk my father's wrath?'

'I am going to tell him what I plan to do,' said Cleo firmly. 'I wouldn't just leave without saying goodbye.'

'Well, good luck with that.' Serena pulled a wry face. 'Though I guess this proves that you're really his granddaughter.' She shook her head. 'Apart from Dominic, we all give in to him, one way or the other.'

She paused. 'But I'll speak to Rick Moreno. He's the pilot who brought you here. He flies into Nassau most days on company business or to pick up supplies. I might be able to arrange with him to take you with him.'

Cleo bit her lip. 'When?'

'When?' Serena frowned. 'Oh—in a day or two.'

'Tomorrow?'

Serena blew out a breath. 'Cleo—'

'Please.'

Serena shook her head. 'I'll do what I can, but I'm not promising anything. Your grandfather may have something to say
about that.'

'Thanks.' Impulsively, Cleo stepped towards her again and
kissed Serena's cheek. 'I appreciate it.'

Serena shook her head. 'I wish you wouldn't do this.' She
sniffed. 'Just as we're getting to know one another.'

Cleo managed a rueful smile. But when she got outside the
room again, and the door was securely closed behind her, she
felt the hot tears rolling down her cheeks.

Dominic was sitting at his desk, staring broodingly into space,
when his cellphone rang.

Flicking it open, he blinked when he saw who was calling
him. The old man always used the office number when he
wanted to get in touch with his grandson there and the very fact
that he hadn't put this call on an entirely different footing.

'Grandpa!' Forcing a neutral tone, Dominic hoped he
sounded less edgy than he felt. 'This is a surprise.'

The old man didn't say anything and Dominic's nerves tightened even more. 'To what do I owe this pleasure?'

'Like you don't know.'

The anger in the older man's voice was almost palpable and
Dominic wearily closed his eyes and dragged a hand down his
face.

'OK,' he said. 'I assume this is about Cleo.'

'You're sharp, I'll give you that.' But Jacob was sarcastic.
'You couldn't keep your hands off her, could you? After the way
you swore to me that you had no intention of ruining her life
as your father ruined her mother's.'

'I haven't.'

But the old man wasn't listening to him. 'Just tell me: did
you sleep with her?'

Dominic heaved a sigh. 'Cleo?'

'Don't mess with me, boy. You know who I mean.'

'OK.' Dominic spoke flatly. 'Yes, I slept with her.'

'Damn you!'

'It's not what you think, old man.'

'No?' Jacob snorted. 'You're going to tell me next that you asked her to marry you. Oh, no, you couldn't do that because marriage isn't on your agenda.'

'Grandpa—'

'You make me sick, do you know that?'

Dominic groaned. 'If you'd let me speak—'

'And say what?'

'That I love her, dammit!' exclaimed Dominic harshly. 'You don't take any prisoners, do you?'

The silence that followed this pronouncement was ominous.

Dominic had expected the old man to say something, even if it was only to call him a liar. But Jacob said nothing, and that was more disturbing than his anger had been.

Unable to sit still while he waited for his grandfather to speak, Dominic pushed himself up from his chair and walked a little jerkily over to the window.

The three-storey block of offices that housed the Montoya Corporation overlooked the bay. A couple of hundred feet above the marina, up a narrow, winding street, it had an unparallelled view of the town and the harbour beyond.

But Dominic was blind to the beauty of his surroundings. Finally, he said, 'Well? Don't you have anything to say?'

'It's too late.'

Jacob's words struck his grandson like a sword to his ribs. 'What do you mean—it's too late?' he snarled. 'I've told you, I love her. I do. I'm going to see her today, to tell her—'

'Well, you should have thought of that sooner.' Jacob was contemptuous. 'But I guess this is all new for you. You don't usually offer marriage to the women you sleep with.'

Dominic bit his tongue on a savage retort. 'This is different,' he muttered. 'I needed time to think.'

'I bet you did.' Jacob snorted. 'Anyway, forget it. It's too late now. She's gone!'

'Cleo?' Dominic felt a sudden chill in the pit of his stomach. 'What the hell are you talking about?'

'I should have thought it was fairly obvious,' said his grandfather coldly. 'She left on this morning's flight.'

'You're kidding!'

'Would I kid about something like that? She's gone, I tell you. She wouldn't listen to anything I had to say. I tried to persuade her to stay on until the end of the two weeks' absence she'd been granted. But it was no use.'

'Jesus!'

'Yes, you might consider calling on Him for forgiveness, boy, because I sure as hell am going to find it hard to forgive you myself.'

Dominic's fist connected with the frame of the window. 'I'll go after her.'

'You won't.' Jacob was very definite about that. 'Don't you think you've done enough damage? She told me she never wants to see you again, and I believe her. If you want to do something useful, I suggest you clear up your own mess. Or is splitting up with Sarah Cordy not so urgent now that the girl you seduced has left the island?'

Dominic sucked in a breath. 'That's a foul accusation to make. Even from you.'

'Yes.' The old man sounded very weary suddenly. 'Yes, it was. And maybe not totally justified. You're a young man. Why shouldn't you sow a few wild oats? I know I did. But you knew how I felt about Cleo. Couldn't you have slaked your lust with someone else?'

'It wasn't lust,' said Dominic doggedly.

'Whatever.' His grandfather's lips turned down. 'It doesn't matter now.'

'It does matter.' Dominic raked frustrated hands through his hair. 'I'll go after her. I'll bring her back. If I tell her how you feel—'

'Do you think, I didn't tell her that?' Jacob was impatient now. 'For goodness' sake, Dominic, I did everything I could to persuade her to stay. But she was determined to leave, and I realise now we have to let her do this. At least for a little while. She's promised me she'll come back if I need her. And I don't want you—especially you—or any of us doing anything to muddy the waters. Do you hear?'

Cleo was standing in the queue at the British Airways check-in desk when someone said her name.

'Cleo?' the woman said, her voice horribly familiar. 'Cleo, are you leaving?'

Cleo hesitated only a moment before turning to face Sarah Cordy.

'Oh, hello,' she said reluctantly. She really didn't want to talk to Dominic's girlfriend at the moment. But politeness necessitated an answer, and with a slight smile she added. 'Yes, I have to get back to London.'

'Really?' Sarah's blue eyes widened. 'This is rather sudden, isn't it? I understood from Dom that you were staying for two weeks.'

'Change of plan,' said Cleo shortly, grateful when the desk clerk chose that moment to ask for her passport. Handing it over, she said, 'Are you going to London, too?'

Hopefully not with Dominic, she appended silently. That would really be too much for her to bear.

'Oh…'

Sarah looked taken aback for a moment. And then, as if a thought had occurred to her, a look of calculation crossed her face.

'Well, no,' she said a little smugly. 'I'm here to meet an associate of Dominic's actually. He asked me to stand in for him. I think he's grooming me for—well, you know.'

Cleo did know. Sarah meant when they were married. She wondered if a heart could split in two.

'Anyway, I think that's the flight that's just landed,' Sarah continued. 'I'd better get going. Enjoy your trip.'

Cleo nodded, but Sarah's departure was hardly a relief.

But then, as she was handed her boarding card, another thought entered her head. If Sarah was here to meet an associate of Dominic's, surely she was in the wrong area of the airport altogether.

She shrugged, and dismissed the thought. What did she know about airports, after all? She'd just be grateful when she was on the flight to London. It was two days since she'd left San Clemente and this was the first available booking she'd been able to make.

CHAPTER FIFTEEN

NORAH met Cleo on the landing outside their small apartment.

It was obvious the other girl had been waiting for her, and Cleo was instantly reminded of that other occasion when Serena Montoya had accosted her at the supermarket.

It was three months since she'd returned to London. Three months and spring had lifted its head at last. There were daffodils in the park and ducks on the pond, and a definite feeling of warmth invading the air.

Not the kind of warmth she'd known when she was in San Clemente, Cleo acknowledged. But England had other attractions for her. A sense of normality for one; a return to the places she was familiar with. The sights and sounds and people she loved.

Of course, she loved her grandfather, too. That realisation had come to her in the darkness of her bedroom and given her some sleepless nights. She worried about him constantly; wished there was some way she could make up to him for the way she'd left the island.

But going to live on San Clemente wasn't an option. She would go and see her grandfather if he needed her, but there was no way she could stay there and constantly come into contact with the man she loved.

Oh, yes. The sudden awareness that she'd felt that night at his house hadn't changed. She loved Dominic. But she would not allow history to repeat itself.

At least she wasn't pregnant.

She'd had a few scary moments, but her period had arrived only two days late that first month home. When she was feeling really low, she conceded it was a mixed blessing. Despite the fact that she told herself she never wanted to see Dominic again, the idea of having his child had been something else.

Was that how her mother had felt? she wondered. Was that why she'd gone ahead and had her child in spite of the obvious difficulties it involved? Had she loved her baby? Cleo felt fairly sure she must have. Which was another reason why she must never forget the past.

Now, as Norah bustled towards the stairhead, she looked at her friend with slightly apprehensive eyes.

'What's wrong?' Cleo asked, her stomach plunging alarmingly. 'Oh, God, it's not my grandfather, is it?'

Norah gave a helpless shrug. 'I don't know why she's here,' she said. 'She wouldn't tell me.'

'She? She?' Cleo's mouth was dry. 'You mean—Serena? Ms Montoya? Is she here?'

Norah shook her head. 'It's not the woman who came before. But I think she did say her name was Montoya.' She spread her hands. 'Anyway, I just wanted to warn you. After the last time…'

Cleo closed her eyes for a moment as they crossed the landing. The urge to turn round and go out again was tempting, but she couldn't leave Norah alone. The trouble was, there were only two other Montoyas it could be: either Dominic had married Sarah, as she'd evidently wanted, or it was Lily. And Cleo was fairly sure it wouldn't be his mother.

But it was.

Amazingly, Lily was seated on their shabby sofa. Despite the warmth of the apartment, she still had her cashmere overcoat clutched about her throat. Perhaps she felt the cold, thought Cleo, trying to distract herself. She couldn't think of a single reason why the woman should be here.

Norah made a beeline for her bedroom. 'I've made some

tea,' she said in passing, indicating the pot standing on the divider. 'If you need anything else, Cleo…'

'Thanks.' Cleo exchanged a look with her friend and then became aware that Lily had risen to her feet as soon as Norah left the room. 'Um—hello, Mrs Montoya. This is a—surprise.'

'A shock, I think.' For once Lily seemed almost approachable. Her smile—a smile Cleo had so rarely seen—came and went in quick succession.

Then, as if she were the hostess, she said, 'Won't you sit down, Cleo? I need to talk to you.' She took a deep breath. 'I've been so worried.'

Although Lily sank onto the sofa once more, Cleo didn't move.

'Grandfather,' she said, scarcely aware that she'd used the familiar form of address. 'I mean—has something happened? Is he worse?' Her voice broke. 'He hasn't—he hasn't—'

'Jacob's fine,' Lily assured her quickly. 'Well, as fine as can be expected, anyway. Isn't that what they always say?' She made an impatient gesture and then, evidently getting tired of looking up at her, she patted the seat beside her. 'Please, sit down, Cleo. You're making me nervous,'

You're making me nervous, thought Cleo, but she obediently loosened her jacket and subsided onto the sofa beside her.

'OK,' she said. 'I'll buy it. What are you worried about?'

Lily regarded her with wary eyes. 'You sound so harsh, my dear. I suppose I'm to blame for that.'

'No one's to blame.' Cleo wasn't about to discuss Dominic with his mother. 'But I am rather tired. It's been a long day.'

'And the last thing you expected was to find me at the end of it?'

Cleo pulled a wry face. 'Frankly, yes.'

'That's understandable.' Lily nodded. Then, glancing towards the kitchen, she said, 'You know, I think I will have a cup of tea, after all.'

Cleo tamped down her resentment and got to her feet.

Whatever was going on here, she wasn't going to find out until Lily was good and ready.

But what could it be? Had Lily found out about her and Dominic? Was she worried that Cleo might be pregnant? That her son might find himself in the same predicament as his father?

She didn't make herself a cup of tea. She simply poured a cup, added milk, and carried it across to Lily. 'Sugar?' she asked, hoping they had some.

But Lily merely shook her head. 'This is good,' she said, taking a sip. 'The English always make the best tea.'

Cleo was tempted to point out that she wasn't English. But it was too much trouble to attempt to justify herself to her.

Resuming her seat, she said, 'Are you going to tell me what all this is about? If you're afraid I might be planning on coming back to live on the island, you can relax. I shall be staying here.'

'Will you?'

Lily's lips twisted, and, although she'd professed herself satisfied with the tea, Cleo noticed she only swallowed a mouthful before setting the cup on the low table at her side.

'I'm hoping I can change your mind,' she went on, causing Cleo to stare at her disbelievingly. 'Oh, yes, my dear. I mean it. For my son's sanity, I think you have to come.'

'Dominic!' His name spilled from Cleo's lips almost automatically. And, despite all the promises she'd made to herself, she felt her heart skip a beat. She took a breath. 'Dominic sent you?'

'Heavens, no! He'd be furious if he knew I was here. Only—only his grandfather knows where I am. Like me, Jacob would do anything for his grandson.'

She pressed her hands together in her lap, breathing rather shallowly. 'I—I'm so afraid he's going to do something terrible to himself, Cleo. He's changed so much since you left. I—I don't think I know him any more.'

Cleo blinked. That was an exaggeration surely.

'I don't understand—'

'His grandfather's worried, too, of course. He blames himself for a lot of what happened.' She paused and then continued with some reluctance, Cleo felt. 'Dom wanted to come after you, you see, but Jacob made him swear he wouldn't do anything without his consent. He insisted you wouldn't want to see him. I think even Jacob thought you'd come round in your own time.'

'Come round?' Cleo gazed at her and Lily nodded.

'You should know,' she said. 'Your grandfather equates everything with money. He was sure the knowledge that you were his legitimate heir would persuade you to come back.'

Cleo gasped. 'I don't care about his money!'

'No. I think he realises that now.' Lily sighed. 'But I'm not here because of Jacob. I want you to know that my son needs you. I never thought I'd say such a thing, but in the circumstances, I don't have a lot of choice.'

Cleo shook her head. 'But what about Sarah?' Her hands were trembling and she trapped them between her shaking knees.

'Oh, well…' Lily was distracted. 'I suppose I hoped something might come of their relationship.' She sighed. 'She's such a lovely girl. And so suitable—'

She broke off abruptly, as if just realising who she was talking to. Then went on, rather heavily, 'But Dominic doesn't love Sarah. According to your grandfather, he loves you…'

She reached for her teacup and managed to raise it to her lips without spilling any, even though her hand was shaking, too.

'Not that he discussed it with anyone,' she went on, her voice wobbling. 'He doesn't discuss his personal feelings at all.' She set her cup down again with a noisy clatter. 'He spends every hour God sends either in that damn plane, flying all over the country, or at the office. We hardly see him. I'm very much afraid he's working himself to death.'

Cleo stared at her. Another exaggeration, she thought, even

as her stomach clenched at the images Lily was creating. 'Dominic has more sense than that.'

'How would you know?' Lily stared at her with resentful eyes. 'You're not his mother. I am.'

Thank goodness for that, thought Cleo, trying desperately to hang on to her own sanity. And that was a thought she'd never have believed she'd have.

'I still don't believe Dominic would do anything foolish,' she said doggedly. 'Surely Sarah—'

'Oh, Sarah's gone away,' said Lily at once. 'The Cordys have family in Miami and I've heard she's staying with them at present.' She hesitated. 'As a matter of fact, she had left the island, but then she came back the next day, apparently all ready to forgive him. I think someone had told her you'd gone back to England, and she must have thought she might still have a chance with him.'

Cleo's jaw dropped.

She was remembering that afternoon when she'd been checking in for her flight to London. She'd wondered why Sarah was in the departure hall when she was supposed to be meeting someone.

My God, Cleo thought now, Sarah had found out she was leaving and taken the next flight back to the island. She'd certainly never mentioned anything about Dominic himself.

Though would she? Cleo asked herself honestly. In Sarah's position, wouldn't she have kept her mouth shut, too? After all, Sarah had evidently wanted Dominic. Cleo guessed she must have been secretly clapping her hands.

'I'm sorry,' she said, but predictably Lily showed little sympathy for the other girl.

'Oh, the Cordys have always coveted Magnolia Hill,' she said carelessly. 'And when Michael had no success with Serena, they set their sights on her nephew instead. I doubt if there was any love involved, my dear, on either side. Even if Sarah's mother and I did encourage people to think there was.

I knew, as soon as I saw you and Dominic together, that you were the one.'

Cleo was stunned. 'I don't believe it.'

'Why not?' Lily's eyes narrowed. 'You are attracted to my son, are you not? It's not a one-sided affair?'

'No.' Cleo bent her head. 'But you don't like me, do you?'

The silence that followed this statement was formidable. Cleo knew she'd gone too far, but for far too long Lily had had it all her own way.

Then, with a little sigh, Lily said, 'I—resented you, Cleo. I admit it. You remind me so much of Celeste. I loved your mother, you know, and she betrayed me. I didn't know about that until Jacob told us what Robert—my husband—had done.'

Cleo drew a tremulous breath. 'I'm sorry.'

'Yes.' Lily lifted her shoulders. 'I was devastated when Celeste died, you know, and her mother took the baby away. Robert told me afterwards that it had died, too, and I had no reason to disbelieve him. I knew nothing about the plans he'd made with the Novaks. That he'd arranged for you to be taken to England with them. The first I heard about it was when Jacob dropped his bombshell. And by the time you arrived, I'd already convinced myself that you were as much to blame as Robert himself.'

Cleo hesitated. 'I've been told that my…father…arranged for me to be adopted by the Novaks because he didn't want to upset you.'

'To upset me!' Lily sounded a little bitter now. 'I fear Robert sent you away to protect himself. Celeste had died, the only witness to his betrayal. He saw a way out of his dilemma that saved him any disgrace and ensured you would always have a comfortable home.'

'But why?' Cleo was confused. 'If no one knew who my father was?'

'You look a lot like him,' said Lily at once. 'He must have seen that immediately. His eyes; his nose; his mouth. Now you even exhibit certain mannerisms he had. He knew I'd have guessed that he was your father and he couldn't allow that.'

'But I thought—because you couldn't have children of your own—'

'We'd adopted Dominic, hadn't we? There was no reason why we shouldn't have adopted you.' Lily sighed. 'My dear girl, that was why he told me you'd died. You see, on top of everything else, you were my half-sister's child.'

Cleo stared. 'I'm afraid I—'

Lily grimaced. 'Robert wasn't the first member of my family to betray his wife, Cleo. Cleopatra Dubois—your grandmother, the person your mother named you after—was my father's mistress many years ago. It was supposed to be a secret. As children, we weren't supposed to know about it. But everybody did. On an island like San Clemente, it's very hard to keep a secret to yourself.'

Cleo could only gaze at her in wonder. 'My father knew this, of course.'

'Of course.' Lily sounded resigned. 'He knew who she was long before she came to live with us. But, after we adopted Dominic, I needed help around the house, someone to look after Dominic when I wasn't there. Celeste offered to be a kind of au pair and I jumped at the chance. We were friends as well as sisters, however unlikely that sounds.'

Cleo was beginning to understand. So many things were slipping into place.

But Lily wasn't quite finished.

'Robert hid his affair with Celeste, as much because *she* didn't want to hurt me as for any sense of guilt he might have felt. Your father was an arrogant man in many ways, Cleo, but I loved him. I prefer not to think about what might have happened if both you and Celeste had survived.'

CHAPTER SIXTEEN

IT WAS strange to be back on San Clemente soil again.

Climbing down from the small aircraft that her grandfather had sent to meet her in Nassau, Cleo looked about her with an odd sense of homecoming.

Which was ridiculous, really. San Clemente had never been her home. Her father had seen to that. And whether her grandfather was right—that Robert had loved both Celeste and his wife and hadn't wanted to hurt Lily—or Lily's story that he was a selfish man who'd been trying to hide his own guilt was the real truth, she would never know.

The fact was, she was beginning to see that she had been an innocent victim of her mother's desires and her father's lust.

The sight of a tall figure, standing in the shade of the airport buildings, drove all other thoughts from her head.

'My God,' she breathed, barely audibly. It was Dominic. Her grandfather had said he would come to meet her himself. What on earth was Dominic doing here?

'You OK, Ms Novak?'

Rick Moreno, the young pilot, had followed her down the steps and was now regarding her with some concern. And Cleo realised she had come to a complete halt, standing there in the brilliant glare of the afternoon sun.

'Oh—er—yes. Yes, I'm fine,' she stammered, managing to put one foot in front of the other, heading somewhat uncertainly for the shelter of the overhang where Dominic was waiting. 'Thanks, Mr Moreno. I think the sun must be getting to me.'

'No problem.'

Rick was carrying the suitcase she'd brought with her, and when he saw Dominic he hailed the other man with a cheerful smile.

'Hey, Mr Montoya,' he said. 'It's good to see you.' He held up the suitcase. 'You got a car I can load this into?'

'Um—Mr Montoya may not have come to meet me,' said Cleo hurriedly, trying not to stare too obviously at Dominic. She glanced around. 'Isn't—isn't Jacob here?'

'No.'

Dominic's response was hardly welcoming, but heavens, Cleo could see why Lily had swallowed her pride and come to find her. If she was to blame for his appearance, she had a lot to answer for.

He looked so gaunt. He'd evidently lost weight, and, although his suit was undoubtedly Armani, the trousers hung loosely from his narrow hips.

'The Roller's over there,' he said, and Rick nodded his understanding. He started in that direction, leaving Cleo and Dominic alone.

Dominic didn't speak and, feeling obliged to make some kind of contact, Cleo said a little awkwardly, 'I thought your grandfather was going to meet me.'

'So did I.'

Once again, Dominic's reply was daunting.

But, gathering her courage, Cleo persisted. 'Well, thanks for coming, anyway,' she murmured. Then, gesturing in Rick's direction, 'Shouldn't we follow him?'

Dominic regarded her without expression. 'What are you doing here, Cleo?' he asked at last. His voice was as cold as an Arctic winter. 'I understood you told the old man that you never wanted to see me again.'

Oh…!

Cleo pulled her lower lip between her teeth. How was she

supposed to answer that? She had said as much, but the circumstances had been so different then.

Lifting her shoulders, she said, 'People change.'

'Do they?' Dominic wasn't convinced. 'Or isn't it a fact that people have their minds changed for them? Particularly if someone lays a guilt trip on them.'

'A guilt trip! No…' Cleo put out her hand to touch his sleeve, but Dominic shifted out of her reach. 'You don't understand.'

'No, I freaking don't,' he agreed harshly. 'But I want you to know that anything my mother has told you is just so much hot air! I don't want you here, Cleo. I don't need you. And if I'm the reason you've swallowed that stubborn pride of yours, then forget it! As far as I'm concerned, you can turn right around and go back where you came from.'

Cleo winced. He'd meant his words to hurt her and they had. But something—the conviction that Lily hadn't been lying, or perhaps the haunted expression in his eyes that, try as he might, he couldn't quite disguise—made her say,

'This is where I came from, Dominic. Don't you remember? You told me that.'

Dominic's jaw clamped. 'Do you think I care what I said to get you here? My grandfather was dying—he *is* dying—and I'd have said anything to get you on that plane. But this…' He made an impatient gesture. 'This is different. If you're here now, it's not because of anything I've said.'

Cleo pressed her lips together for a moment. This was going to be so much harder than she'd ever imagined. If she didn't know better, she'd have said he hated her. Perhaps he did hate her. After all, hatred was akin to love.

With a supreme effort, she pasted a smile on her lips. 'Well, we'll just have to see, won't we?' she said, in much the same tone as she'd have used to a child. 'Shall we get going?'

'Don't patronise me, Cleo.'

'I wouldn't dream of it,' she said pleasantly. She turned to the young pilot who had deposited his load and was now approaching. 'Thanks again, Mr Moreno. You're a star.'

Rick grinned at her, but then, seeing his employer's glowering expression, he quickly sobered. 'No problem, Ms Novak,' he said. He nodded politely at Dominic. 'I'll be flying out later tonight, Mr Montoya. Will you be needing me tomorrow?'

'I'll let you know.'

Dominic was abrupt and he immediately despised himself for taking his ill humour out on the other man. During the past few weeks, he and Rick had flown together many times, and the young pilot was always good-tempered and polite.

'Yes, sir.'

Rick executed a salute and then disappeared through the door that led into the terminal building to register his arrival. And, because she guessed their behaviour was being monitored by the airport staff, Cleo headed determinedly towards where the ancient Rolls-Royce convertible that her grandfather was so proud of was waiting.

Rick had stowed her suitcase in the boot. And after tossing her hand luggage into the back seat, Cleo pulled open the passenger door and tucked herself inside.

Dominic walked round the vehicle to the driver's side, yanking open the door and coiling his length behind the wheel. The sleeve of his jacket brushed her bare arm as he did so, and she wondered how he could bear to wear a suit on a day like this.

A faint smell of soap invaded the car at his entrance, and she noticed that the ends of dark hair that brushed his collar at the back were wet. He'd evidently had a shower, either at the house or at his office. Though, judging by the growth of stubble on his chin, he hadn't stopped to shave.

Even so, she felt a warm feeling inside her at the thought that he'd made an effort on her behalf. It sort of contradicted his assertion that he wanted her to leave. At once.

Or was she just clutching at straws?

She still hadn't the first idea how she was going to handle this. Was she even capable of doing so? Lily might have confidence in her abilities, but she had no confidence at all.

Taking a deep breath, she glanced his way. She had to get a conversation going, she thought as he drove out of the terminal parking area. She had to try and get him talking before they reached Magnolia Hill and he could abandon her without another word.

Clearing her throat, she said, 'Aren't you too hot? I mean, I assume you've been to the office, but do you really need your jacket on?'

'Do you really think it's any of your business?' he countered, checking the traffic. Then, with a mocking twist to his mouth, 'I bet you got the shock of your life when my mother turned up at your door.'

'How do you—?'

Cleo broke off, realising what she was admitting to, and Dominic's expression hardened at the obvious slip.

'How do I know she came to see you?' he remarked at last, taking pity on her. 'She told me herself. I think she hoped I'd be impressed.'

'And, of course, you weren't,' said Cleo tersely, resenting his superiority. 'Anyway, she was worried about you,' she added. 'Apparently she never sees you these days.'

'Well, she must have been worried to have got in touch with you,' he said, and Cleo caught her breath at the callousness of his words.

'Gee, thanks,' she said, trying not to show how small that made her feel. 'Well, I guess I was the last resort.'

Dominic scowled. Despite the way he felt about her—and right now he wished her any place else but here—he didn't like hurting her.

Dammit!

Not that she didn't deserve his contempt, he reminded himself savagely. She'd practically robbed him of any desire for living. And that was a heavy burden to shift.

'Look,' he said wearily, 'let's not pretend you wanted to come back here. And don't for a minute imagine that I knew in advance what my mother intended to do. I didn't. And if I had known, I'd have stopped her. Why can't she just leave me alone to get on with my life?'

'With your death, your mean!' exclaimed Cleo passionately, and Dominic gave her an incredulous look. 'Well, it's true,' she went on. 'What are you doing to yourself?' Her voice broke on a sob. 'What have I done to you?'

The car braked abruptly, and the small pick-up that had been following them along the coast road skidded wildly, almost swerving over the cliff.

The driver raised an angry fist as he went by, but Dominic wasn't paying him any attention. His eyes were fixed on Cleo's tormented face, and when she looked up and met his furious gaze, he shook his head.

'Oh, boy, she really did a number on you, didn't she?' he exclaimed. 'What the hell has she been saying? It must have been something pretty drastic to bring you back to San Clemente.'

Cleo fumbled in her pocket for a tissue. But she'd stuffed her denim jacket into her hand luggage before leaving the plane. Her sleeveless T-shirt and tight jeans left little room for extras.

Finally, abandoning her search, she rubbed her nose with the back of her hand. Then she ventured unevenly, 'I wanted to come back. I've wanted to come back every day since I left here.'

'Yeah, right.' Dominic was sardonic. Then, leaning forward, he rummaged in the glove compartment and pulled out a small pack of tissues.

He handed them to her and she was shocked to find his fingers were icy. 'You're good, Cleo, I'll give you that,' he said, his smile as cold as his flesh. 'Who came up with that explanation? No, don't tell me. It was my mother.'

Cleo felt the prick of tears behind her eyes. 'It wasn't your mother,' she retorted tightly. 'It's not made up. If—if you'd only listen to what I have to say—'

'Oh, yeah. And I'm supposed to believe that you were only waiting for an invitation to come back?'

'Not an invitation, no.' Cleo sighed. He was so hard; so un-forgiving. 'Can't you at least try and look at things from my side for a change?'

'Why should I?' Dominic's expression darkened. 'You've got a bloody nerve, coming here, expecting me to feel sympathy for you. I didn't ask you to come back. And you've only got my mother's word that I'd even want to lay eyes on you again.'

'Oh, Dominic!'

Cleo gazed at him with tear-wet eyes. She wouldn't have believed he could be so cruel. And the disturbing notion that Lily might have been wrong in her interpretation of events hit her with a mind-numbing blow.

'You—you have to understand how I felt when I left here,' she ventured huskily. 'All right. We'd slept together, and that was—that was amazing—'

Dominic's disbelieving gaze turned in her direction for a second, but then he forced himself to resume his contemplation of the ocean.

She didn't mean that, he assured himself. This was just another ploy on his mother's part to try and control his life.

'—but I—I couldn't be your mistress.'

Dominic's eyes raked her anxious face again. 'Had I asked you to be my mistress?' he demanded savagely. 'You'd better refresh my memory. I don't remember that at all.'

'No.' Cleo groaned. 'No, you hadn't actually said that—'

'Thank heaven for small mercies!' He was sarcastic.

'—but—but I was sure that was what you wanted.'

'Really?' He stared at her now, his eyes dark and dangerous. 'And you presumed to know my mind about this, just as you presumed to know better than me that night at Turtle Cove, right?'

Cleo blew out a nervous breath. 'I've explained about that.'

'Have you?'

'Yes.' Her tongue circled her lips. 'Can't you see I'm strug-gling here? I thought—I thought I had to get away from you before…before I did something I'd regret.'

'Like going to bed with me again?' Dominic's mouth curled. 'Yeah, I can see how that might have been a problem for you.'

'Oh, don't be so stupid!' Cleo glared at him through her tears. 'I was in love with you, all right? And I was afraid of getting hurt.' She pressed her palms to her hot cheeks. 'You can blame my mother, if you like, but that was the problem.'

Dominic's eyes darkened. 'Why would you think I'd hurt you?'

'Because of Sarah,' she answered simply. 'I thought you might be planning on marrying Sarah, and I couldn't have borne to live with that.'

Dominic was steeling himself against the urge to comfort her. Her tears tore him apart, but he still couldn't ignore what Sarah had said…

'So how do you explain what you said to Sarah at Nassau Airport?' he asked harshly.

'Sarah?' Cleo blinked, scrubbing the heels of her hands across her cheeks. 'What am I supposed to have said?'

'You didn't happen to tell her that you hoped you'd never see me again?'

'Or course not.' Cleo was horrified.

'But you don't deny you had a conversation with her?'

'It was hardly a conversation,' protested Cleo. 'And your name wasn't even mentioned. Oh—except when she told me you'd sent her to meet some business colleague of yours, but that was—'

'Say what?'

Dominic's expression was incredulous now and suddenly Cleo realised that her suspicions about the other girl were all true.

'There was no business colleague, was there?' she breathed. 'Your mother told me Sarah had left the island, but I didn't put it all together.'

'Put what together?'

'The fact that she wanted me to think you two were still a couple.'

'But how could you think that?' Dominic was struggling not to allow the feeling of euphoria that was building inside him to take control. 'You saw what happened between me and Sarah. Dammit, you must have heard something when you were hiding out in the bushes beneath my deck.'

'I wasn't hiding out in the bushes,' murmured Cleo unhappily. She shook her head. 'Oh—I'm no good at this at all.'

'You're better than me,' muttered Dominic, half turning in his seat towards her. 'I should have known Jacob's sudden frailty was too convenient. I guess he knows how weak and vulnerable I am.'

Dominic, weak and vulnerable?

Cleo didn't believe it. His brooding profile was very dear, but also very remote.

She wanted to reach out to him; to plunge her fingers into the silky dampness of his hair; to cradle his solemn face between her palms and make him see that her life wouldn't be worth living if he wasn't in it.

But she wasn't that courageous.

There was silence for a long time and then Dominic said softly, 'So you came back because my mother put the fear of God into you.'

'No.' Cleo held up her head. 'I came back because she convinced me you needed me.'

'And do you still think I do?'

'I don't know what to think,' she confessed huskily. 'But—but now I've seen you—'

'Yes?'

'—I think she might have had a point.'

Dominic grimaced. 'I look that bad, hmm?'

And suddenly, she couldn't take any more.

Uncaring what he thought, she reached out and grabbed the hair at the back of his neck, jerking him towards her. Then she recklessly pressed her mouth to his.

It was the first time she'd ever done such a thing, but she knew she had to do something to break through his iron control.

And, although his lips were only warm to begin with, they quickly heated beneath the sensuous pressure of hers.

She heard Dominic utter a savage protest, but the chemistry between them was undeniable. Despite any lingering resentment he might feel because of her prolonged absence, the instantaneous hunger of his own response made any kind of resistance futile.

'Dammit, Cleo,' he said hoarsely, and then his hands came almost convulsively to grip her shoulders, and he took control of the kiss.

Crushing her back against the leather squabs, he angled his mouth so that he could plunder the sweet cavity of hers with his tongue.

Her tongue came to meet his, a writhing, sensuous mating that gave as much as it took. And Dominic felt the anger he'd been nurturing all these weeks dissolving beneath the delicious vulnerability of her warm body.

Cleo's own relief was overwhelming. She'd been so afraid he wouldn't forgive her. Winding her arms about his neck, she pressed herself as close as the central console would allow.

But it wasn't close enough.

Finding the collar of his jacket, she pushed it off his shoulders, relieved to find that his skin was now much warmer to her touch. But she wanted to be even nearer and her fingers fumbled frantically with the buttons on his shirt.

Dominic sucked in a tortured breath when he felt her hands on his body, and his mouth dived urgently for the sensitive curve of her neck.

He felt hungry, feverish, and when she gave a little moan of pleasure he felt his own needs threatening to explode inside him.

'We have got to get out of here,' he muttered, covering her face with hot, addictive kisses. His hands slid down her arms to find the provocative thrust of her breasts, and he longed to tear the T-shirt over her head.

He wanted to touch her, much more intimately than their

present situation would allow. And, although right now he was crazy enough not to care, she meant so much more to him than a tumble in the back seat of his grandfather's car.

Pushing her back into the seat, he shrugged out of his jacket and tossed it into the back seat. Suddenly he was sweating, and it was such a good feeling.

'Where are we going?' asked Cleo, half-afraid he was going to take her to Magnolia Hill, and Dominic gave her a wry look as he started the car.

'Well, not to see your grandfather,' he said a little ruefully. 'The old devil can stew for a bit longer.'

'What do you mean?'

Cleo looked at him, her dark brows raised, and Dominic's foot pressed harder on the accelerator.

'He knew what he was doing when he asked me to come and meet you,' he said drily. 'He swore he was too tired to make the trip himself. And Serena was conveniently absent.'

'And did you mind?'

'Yes, I minded,' said Dominic honestly. 'He knew how I felt about you, and I couldn't conceive of any way you might want to see me again.'

'Dominic!'

'It's true.' He grimaced. 'I thought you'd come back because of something my mother had said. And I didn't want your— pity.'

'My pity!' Cleo caught her breath. 'Oh, darling…'

Dominic let out a tortured breath. 'Anyway, naturally he didn't want to ask Lily again, so—I was his only option. Or so he said.'

'Thank God!'

Cleo's response was fervent and, spreading her fingers over his thigh, she squeezed provocatively.

Dominic almost choked then. 'Please,' he said hoarsely, 'don't do that.'

'Why?' Cleo's smile was mischievous. 'Don't you like it?'

'I'll answer that when we get to Turtle Cove,' said Dominic, his look promising a delicious retribution, and Cleo shivered in delight.

The journey seemed to take forever. But at last Dominic turned between the stone gates that marked the extent of his property and drove swiftly up to the house.

They left the car on the forecourt, where a fountain sparkled brilliantly in the late-afternoon sun. But even before they reached the entry, Cleo was in Dominic's arms.

Ambrose, Dominic's houseman, appeared briefly in the open doorway, but he quickly made himself scarce. He could see his employer had everything he wanted for the moment, and his smile was a sign of his satisfaction, too.

They paused in the foyer only long enough for Dominic to haul Cleo's T-shirt over her head and to shed his own shirt. Then with his mouth still on hers they stumbled along the corridor to his bedroom.

Cleo thought it was odd seeing the place in daylight, but it was just as beautiful as she remembered. Dominic was just as beautiful, too, and her head swam as, between more of those soul-draining kisses, they peeled one another's clothes off.

Then he tumbled her onto the bed, and she felt his hot, aroused body between her legs.

'I want you—so much,' he muttered in a husky, impassioned voice.

And with her body throbbing with the uncontrolled hunger only he could assuage, Cleo gave herself up to the physical needs of passion…

EPILOGUE

CLEO'S hair was still damp.

A silky strand was lying on the pillow beside Dominic's head and he coiled it round his finger.

It was so dark; even darker than his own, with a bluish tinge that gave it a lustrous vitality. It was so essentially her, and he loved it.

He loved everything about her, he thought, bringing the strand of hair to his lips. He inhaled, smelling his shampoo, and he liked the intimacy of that, too.

After their first frantic coupling, they'd taken a shower together. And he'd delighted in soaping her hair and her body, in covering every inch of her skin with his scent.

But, despite the smell of expensive lotions, he could still smell himself on her, and that pleased him.

It was hardly surprising, after all. Rubbing his hands all over her had aroused them both once again, and they'd made love beneath the cooling spray of water. He had pinned Cleo against the wall of the cubicle, and she'd wound her legs around his hips.

Amazingly, they'd made love again when they'd got back into bed. Dominic hadn't known he had it in him, but just thinking of making love with Cleo made him harden with desire.

She was the woman he loved, his soulmate; and he was

never going to let her go. They belonged together; they always had. And he could even feel grateful to his grandfather: without the old man's intervention, he might never have known her.

Cleo was sleeping now.

She was probably exhausted, he reflected. He was pretty tired, too. But he didn't want to miss a minute of the bliss in knowing they were together at last. He'd have plenty of time for sleep when they were married.

Married!

Cleo Montoya. He experimented with the name. Mrs Dominic Montoya. Yeah, that sounded really good.

It was getting dark outside, but he hadn't bothered to close the curtains. If anyone—his mother, Serena or his grandfather—chose to come and peer in at his windows, he really didn't care. He had nothing to hide, nothing to be ashamed of. He and Cleo were a couple.

And how amazing was that!

He stirred and Cleo's eyes flickered. Long, silky lashes lifted, and then she turned her head and encountered his gaze.

'What time is it?' she asked sleepily, and Dominic pulled her closer.

'About six,' he said softly. 'Are you hungry? I can have Ambrose fix us something to eat.'

Cleo's lips parted, and a dreamy expression entered her eyes. 'Is this really happening?' she whispered. 'Are we really together? This isn't just a dream, is it?'

'If it is, I'm having the same dream,' said Dominic, nuzzling her shoulder. 'No, sweetheart, it's not a dream. You're here, at Turtle Cove. In my bed.'

'Hmm, I like that,' she murmured, loving the feel of his stubble against her skin. 'But I suppose I'll have to go and see...*our*... grandfather. He must be wondering what's going on.'

'Oh, I think he has a fair idea,' said Dominic drily. 'I must have convinced all of them that I was in love with you. Why else would my mother have swallowed her pride and gone to see you?'

'Do you think he was worried?' asked Cleo anxiously. 'I wouldn't like to think I was to blame for any relapse in his condition.'

Dominic grinned. 'If Grandpa was worried, it was only over his part in the situation,' he said firmly. 'He was so sure you'd realise what you were giving up—financially, I mean—and come back.'

'But I never wanted his money!'

'Well, he knows that now,' agreed Dominic. 'And I dare say it did him good to sweat for a while.'

Cleo hesitated. 'But he is all right, isn't he?'

'He's OK.' Dominic was reflective. 'No one really knows how his condition will develop.'

Cleo drew a trembling breath. 'Well, I'm glad I'm going to see him again. I realised—I'm very fond of him.'

'That's good to know.' Dominic's eyes darkened. 'And how about me?'

Cleo gazed at him with her heart in her eyes. 'You know I love you,' she breathed. 'So much. That was why I had to go away. I couldn't bear the thought of seeing you and Sarah together.'

Dominic deposited a kiss on her nose. 'There was no way I could have married Sarah feeling as I do about you,' he said solemnly.

'No, but there were so many similarities between our relationship and that of my mother and father. I was afraid of what might happen next.'

'That you might get pregnant? You're not, are you?' he asked, raising his brows, and she giggled.

'Not yet,' she conceded, happily, and he pulled a wry face.

'Well, that's OK, I guess,' he said after a moment. 'I would like to have you to myself for a little while first.'

Cleo touched his cheek. 'I don't deserve you.'

'No.' Dominic grinned. 'But I'll forgive you.'

There was silence in the room for a few delicious moments and then Cleo stirred again.

'You know,' she said softly, 'Lily told me that Celeste was really her half-sister. Did you know that?'

'Hell, no!' Dominic was amused. 'Well, what do you know? My maternal grandfather wasn't as uptight as he liked people to think.'

Cleo nodded. 'Your mother said that my father wasn't the first male to be infatuated with the Dubois women.'

'And he's not the last,' Dominic reminded her staunchly. He bent and nipped the corner of her mouth with his teeth. 'Don't forget, you're a Dubois, too.'

'I haven't forgotten.'

'But there is a difference,' said Dominic, frowning, and Cleo felt a twinge of apprehension.

'What kind of a difference?'

'Well, I'm going to have the distinction of marrying a Dubois woman, if she'll have me.'

He touched her lips with his thumb. 'Will you have me, Cleo? Will you complete the circle and become my wife?'

And, of course, Cleo said yes.

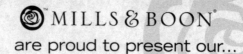

MILLS & BOON
are proud to present our...

Book of the Month

Snowbound: Miracle Marriage
by Sarah Morgan from
Mills & Boon® Medical™

Confirmed bachelor Dr Daniel Buchannan is
babysitting his brother's children and needs help!
Stella, his ex-fiancée, reluctantly rescues him and,
snowbound with his makeshift family, Daniel
realises he can never let Stella go again…

Enjoy double the romance in this
great-value 2-in-1!
Snowbound: Miracle Marriage
&
Christmas Eve: Doorstep Delivery
by Sarah Morgan

Mills & Boon® Medical™
Available 4th December 2009

Something to say about our
Book of the Month?
Tell us what you think!
millsandboon.co.uk/community

millsandboon.co.uk Community

Join Us!

The Community is the perfect place to meet and chat to kindred spirits who love books and reading as much as you do, but it's also the place to:

- **Get the inside scoop from authors about their latest books**
- **Learn how to write a romance book with advice from our editors**
- **Help us to continue publishing the best in women's fiction**
- **Share your thoughts on the books we publish**
- **Befriend other users**

Forums: Interact with each other as well as authors, editors and a whole host of other users worldwide.

Blogs: Every registered community member has their own blog to tell the world what they're up to and what's on their mind.

Book Challenge: We're aiming to read 5,000 books and have joined forces with The Reading Agency in our inaugural Book Challenge.

Profile Page: Showcase yourself and keep a record of your recent community activity.

Social Networking: We've added buttons at the end of every post to share via digg, Facebook, Google, Yahoo, technorati and de.licio.us.

www.millsandboon.co.uk

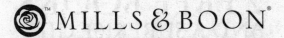

2 FREE BOOKS
AND A SURPRISE GIFT

We would like to take this opportunity to thank you for reading this Mills & Boon® book by offering you the chance to take TWO more specially selected books from the Modern™ series absolutely FREE! We're also making this offer to introduce you to the benefits of the Mills & Boon® Book Club™—

- **FREE home delivery**
- **FREE gifts and competitions**
- **FREE monthly Newsletter**
- **Exclusive Mills & Boon Book Club offers**
- **Books available before they're in the shops**

Accepting these FREE books and gift places you under no obligation to buy, you may cancel at any time, even after receiving your free books. Simply complete your details below and return the entire page to the address below. You don't even need a stamp!

YES Please send me 2 free Modern books and a surprise gift. I understand that unless you hear from me, I will receive 4 superb new books every month for just £3.19 each, postage and packing free. I am under no obligation to purchase any books and may cancel my subscription at any time. The free books and gift will be mine to keep in any case.

Ms/Mrs/Miss/Mr_____ Initials _____

_____

Surname _____

Address _____

_____

_____ Postcode _____

Send this whole page to: Mills & Boon Book Club, Free Book Offer, FREEPOST NAT 10298, Richmond, TW9 1BR